# The Ultimate

## K.A. Applegate

AN
**APPLE**
PAPERBACK

SCHOLASTIC INC.
New York Toronto London Auckland Sydney
Mexico City New Delhi Hong Kong

Cover illustration by David B. Mattingly
Art Direction/Design by Karen Hudson/Ursula Albano

ISBN 0-439-11524-8

12 11 10 9 8 7 6 5 4 3 2 1          1 2 3 4 5 6/0

Printed in the U.S.A.
First Scholastic printing, February 2001

The author wishes to thank Kimberly Morris for
her help in preparing this manuscript.

And for Michael and Jake

# The Ultimate

# CHAPTER 1

Tsseeeewww! Tsseeeewww!

I dropped to the ground. Dracon fire narrowly missed frying my head. Before the enemy could squeeze off another round, I rolled into one of the newly dug trenches.

The trench was muddy, the soil teeming with earthworms. Gross, but it was protection. And the trench was deep enough for me to morph big. But under an attack like this, I knew to go small.

Tsseeeewww! Tsseeeewww!

More Dracon fire whizzed by overhead. And then I heard the sound that always makes my blood run cold.

Like somebody sharpening knives. Stalking me. Preparing to kill.

It's a sound I seriously don't enjoy.

The sound of Hork-Bajir.

Hork-Bajir are massive creatures. Seven feet tall with machete-like blades on their elbows, their knees, and their foreheads. They're not natural diggers, like the Taxxons. But they can move a powerful amount of earth if they have to.

"Hrrath!"

Tsseeeewww!

A shout and another round of Dracon fire. The whisking, knife-sharpening sound receded slightly. I poked my head above the rim of the trench. Saw Marco running across the compound yard, another group of Hork-Bajir close behind him.

He was creating a diversion. Helping me to escape. Giving me time to morph.

Marco dove into another trench.

I knew what to do. We'd planned it in advance. Rehearsed it endlessly.

We'd use our roach morphs to escape the compound through a network of underground pipes we'd laid beneath the trenches.

I closed my eyes to begin the morph. From ground level, more shouts and explosions. Were my parents out there, vulnerable to the attack? Terrified?

The morph was slow to start. I couldn't con-

2

centrate. *Fix the image of the roach in your mind, Cassie. Fix it and morph.*

No use. I couldn't keep the roach within view. Instead, I saw my mother.

Saw the look on her face when, for the very first time, she watched me morph.

What would her face look like now if she saw me burrowing in a muddy trench full of worms, dung, and rotted vegetation?

*Stop it!* I ordered myself. You have to do this! So, do it.

I concentrated hard. Nothing. I couldn't morph. And I'm the one who's supposed to be so good at it.

<Cassie! Come on! Where are you?> Marco.

I concentrated harder. Now it was my dad's face that appeared in my mind. He looked sad and disappointed. As if until this moment he'd never realized that evil really did exist. Not only in the big "out there." But right in his own backyard.

The Hork-Bajir were closing in. I could hear their blades slicing the air. It was now or never.

If only I could know my parents had taken cover, reached safety!

<Morph, Cassie!>

Jake's voice, commanding me through thought-speak.

3

I looked up. Two Hork-Bajir were staring down at me. Jaws open, blades gleaming. One of them reached to scoop away the muddy soil. To grab me.

That did it. I flattened myself against the bottom of the trench, facedown. Felt earthworms tickling my skin. I fought the urge to puke and started the morph.

Crrreeeeek!

Fingernails turned brown, then crept up along the backs of my hands. Covering them with a hard, shiny brown skin. Then that new skin spread up my arms and across my back. Worked its way over my belly and down my legs.

My skin, once supple, was now the hard exoskeleton matter of a roach.

One of the Hork-Bajir said something. I couldn't understand the words. A roach's sense of hearing isn't great. But the roach could easily sense vocal vibrations. And movement.

Whumpf! Whumpf!

A massive Hork-Bajir talon scraped the soil around me. *Faster.* I willed the human-sized roach to shrink to less than an inch long. Small enough to slip between huge Hork-Bajir claws.

The other Hork-Bajir stepped down into the trench.

Whumpf!

I felt the vibrations of a heavy footfall. But I

4

was safe. The morph was complete. The roach crawled down deep, into the soft, squishy mud.

Suddenly, the smell of pepper and cinnamon and oregano.

Perfect.

A spice sack, planted at the opening of each pipe to guide the roach to the escape path.

Scraaaape. Scraaaape.

The soil above me ruptured as the Hork-Bajir continued to claw at the mud. But I'd reached the narrow opening of the pipe.

Once inside, I ran. Skimmed along the slick interior, easily following the narrow twists and turns.

The tunnel swooped gently upward. I hurried up the incline. Finally, daylight. I emerged and began to demorph.

With a rapid series of disturbing motions my human self began to emerge from the tiny insect body. When the demorph was complete, I stumbled to my bare feet.

And stood before a gorilla, a Siberian tiger, and a grizzly bear.

Marco, Jake, and Rachel.

Already in battle morphs.

Ax and Tobias were on the other side of the camp. At least that was where they were supposed to be, according to the plan.

The plan. Well, basically, if there was ever a

surprise attack by the Yeerks, we would escape the compound as roaches, demorph, go to battle morphs, circle the camp, and go back in to fight.

<Where have you been?!> Jake demanded. <Seconds count, Cassie. You know that.>

Before I could answer, there was a crashing in the brush and two Hork-Bajir cut their way through the trees.

We stood in the clearing. Defenseless. No escape.

The smaller Hork-Bajir stepped forward. In her slightly guttural speech, she announced, "You are all dead. And so is everyone in the compound."

# CHAPTER 2

<Thanks, Toby,> Jake said dryly.

The leader of the free Hork-Bajir bowed her head.

"I'm not criticizing," she said. "Your plan is a good one. But only if everybody cooperates. It's a good thing this was just a war game."

Jake, Rachel, and Marco began to demorph. When he was human again, Jake gave me an odd look.

"The plan depends on rapid response and following orders. Where were you, Cassie? And why did you demorph before I gave you the safe signal?"

Good question. I'd forgotten we weren't supposed to come out of roach morph unless Jake gave us the okay.

If we came out of the pipe and didn't hear Jake's private thought-speak, it meant that we should keep out of sight. Wait for further instructions.

I felt my face get hot. "Sorry."

Jake shrugged and turned to Toby. "What about the others? Did any of them get it right?"

Toby hesitated. "Well, let's just hope the Yeerks don't launch an attack any time soon. The adult humans need much drilling. Or else they will need a lot of protection."

I guess it's time to explain a few things. Like why a seemingly average kid was diving into mud and crawling through pipes. As a roach.

My name is Cassie.

At first there were only five of us. Just five ordinary kids. Until one evening we hooked up at the mall and decided to walk home together. Through an abandoned construction site.

Mistake number one.

Because that's where we stumbled on a crashed spaceship. And an alien named Elfangor.

And ended up in this war.

The pilot was close to death. Before he died he told us an amazing but true story. That Earth had been invaded by Yeerks, parasitic, sentient sluglike things that had been infesting bodies of various species around the galaxy. Now the Yeerks were on our planet. Busily invading the human race. Taking human bodies as their hosts.

Elfangor also gave us a small blue box. A cube that held the key to the most valuable piece of technology his people, the Andalites, had ever developed.

The ability to morph.

That was the beginning.

Later, we were joined by another Andalite. Aximili-Esgarrouth-Isthill. Ax. A cadet in training. A kid like us.

Like we were, once. Because none of us will ever really be kids again.

Now, a hundred or more battles later, I'm not sure exactly what we are. In the eyes of the innocent world, we're still children. But in our own eyes . . .

We've won some of those battles. Lost others. At least we've come out alive. But the war rages on.

And everything is different. Because now, the Yeerks know we're not "Andalite bandits." Now they know we're human. Most of us, anyway. They even know our names. They know who our families are, too.

Which meant we had to tell our families everything. About the Yeerks. About the Andalites.

About why we call ourselves Animorphs. About the months of fighting and the incredible danger and the exhausting emotional drain.

We didn't have time to break the news to our families gently. Not with the Yeerks on the way. We had to evacuate our homes — our lives — immediately.

Just about all of our parents are still in shock. Who can blame them? Even after everything I've witnessed, after everything I've done and had done to me, sometimes I can't believe it's real, either. Sometimes I just know that at any minute I'll wake up from this nightmare.

So now we're in hiding. Me and my parents. Rachel, her mom, and her sisters. Her father lives in another state. There was no time to find him.

Marco and his parents are here, too. Tobias and his long-lost mother, Loren.

Everyone except for Jake's parents. And brother.

We're taking refuge with the colony of free Hork-Bajir. So far, the Yeerks haven't found this new camp. For now at least, we're safe.

The Hork-Bajir are by nature gentle tree-dwellers. And, well, by our human standards, not too bright. But Toby, their "seer," is different. She's done a good job of leading her people. Keeping them safe on a daily basis. Trouble-shooting in emergencies.

Toby and Jake discussed logistics as we walked back to camp.

"The trenches need to be at least eight feet deeper," she said. "And the escape pipes need to be imbedded in concrete to keep them from shifting."

"What if they fill up with water?"

"That's an easy problem to fix," Toby answered.

Jake nodded. But he didn't ask any more questions. Like how Toby planned to fix flooding pipes. And how long it would take. And could Taxxons dig up the pipes, concrete or no concrete.

That wasn't like Jake. Jake was usually way in front of any situation.

The truth was, and it hurt me to admit it, Jake just wasn't Jake anymore.

# CHAPTER 3

Jake's parents, Jean and Steve, didn't make it out in time.

Their chances of escape were slim from the beginning.

See, Jake's older brother, Tom, has been a human-Controller since the early days of the invasion. Even with the enemy under his own roof, Jake had managed to protect his parents from the Yeerks. And from their own son, their own first child.

Because Tom wouldn't have hesitated to kill either one of his parents if the Yeerk mission required their deaths.

Jake had done an almost superhuman job of

protecting his parents. Both from death and a fate worse than death.

Infestation.

Until the last time. When the Yeerks finally took them.

Jake hasn't been the same since. He blames himself.

Yeah, he goes through the motions. But it's like he's lost the spark. Lost whatever it was that kept him going.

That kept us going.

We got back to the camp. Ax and Tobias came wandering in from their positions.

Tobias was in human form. These days, his human self is an acquired morph. Made possible by a powerful, enigmatic being called the Ellimist. Since the very first battle we fought, Tobias's natural form has been red-tailed hawk.

Tobias is a *nothlit.* Someone who stayed in morph beyond the two-hour time limit and got trapped in that morph.

None of us are one hundred percent sure it was an accident.

Sometimes we think Tobias is happier as a hawk. That he let himself be trapped, on purpose.

But none of us has come right out and asked him. At least, I haven't.

And none of us has asked if given the same

situation he'd do it again. Assuming Tobias chose his fate and wasn't just a victim of a really bad circumstance.

Anyway, Rachel was upset.

"That was a disaster! People, we've got to get it together." She turned to Jake. "Well? Aren't you going to *do* something?"

Jake rubbed his hand over his face. He looked exhausted. "If I knew what to do," he said between gritted teeth, "I would be doing it."

Marco stuck his fingers in his mouth and produced a loud "break-it-up" whistle. "Time out. Look, we're all on the same page here. We just need a little more practice. Tomorrow. Let's call it a day."

Still, Marco waited until Jake nodded. Then he walked off toward the cabin the Hork-Bajir had helped his parents construct.

Rachel turned to Jake. "You're letting him walk off like that?"

Jake lifted his hand . . . and dropped it. Like he didn't have the energy to argue. Then he, too, walked away.

Rachel turned to me with that no-tolerance look in her eyes. "If we don't get serious and focus . . ."

I tuned out. Rachel's my best friend. She always puts the mission first. Which is a good thing in a fighter.

But sometimes she has trouble cutting an

individual, a person, slack. She's not cruel, just . . . hard sometimes.

I let her rage on. Everybody had gone back to work now that the drill was over. Hork-Bajir and humans worked on the structures that would house any new arrivals to the camp. The thumping and buzzing of hammers, axes, and saws made it easier to ignore Rachel's voice.

But it didn't block out another familiar voice. My mom, arguing with a Hork-Bajir workman. I left Rachel, still complaining, and hurried over to her. The Hork-Bajir used my arrival to get back to his task.

"Mom! You and dad were supposed to take cover. You know, the drill? All the training? What happened?"

She shook her head dismissively. Like she had something way more important to discuss. "Cassie, we've got to do something."

"What's the matter?"

She pointed to the long, low, windowless structure behind us. The place where the children, elderly, and ill would take refuge in case of a real surprise attack.

It was a rock-and-wood fortress. No windows. Just little holes through which those who were strong enough could fire what weapons we had accumulated.

Several Hork-Bajir were covering the struc-

15

ture with mud. Spackling up the cracks and covering the roof with vines so the structure couldn't be easily spotted from the air.

"Look at that," my mother said angrily.

"Mom, I'm not getting it. What's wrong?"

She put her hands on her hips. "Cassie. Fifty, sixty Hork-Bajir might all have to live in that structure."

"Only if we're under siege," I explained patiently. "And not for a long time. Hopefully."

My mother shook her head again. As if what I'd said didn't make any sense.

"I don't care *why* they'll be living there." She held up three fingers. "One: There's no ventilation except for some tiny squares in the wall. Two: The provisions for sanitation are practically nonexistent. Three: An animal the size of a Hork-Bajir needs at least forty square feet of —"

I cut her off. "Mom! The Hork-Bajir are not animals."

"Cassie, just let me —"

"Okay, they're not humans, but they're not big pets, either. The Hork-Bajir are a sentient species. They're capable of understanding what's in their own best interests. Just like humans."

"I understand that," Mom said in an exasperated tone. "Although I'm not sure I totally agree. But Cassie, you don't seem to understand my point. If a group of Hork-Bajir spend any prolonged time in those conditions, they could easily die."

Suddenly, unexpectedly, I was angry. Mad that my mother, a scientist, wouldn't — or couldn't — face the awful truth.

That we were at war. That the rules had changed. That we had to do things we'd never choose to do under peacetime circumstances. That we didn't have that luxury. That every single minute of every single day we had to make sacrifices we'd rather not make.

And I was angry that my mother was forcing me to confront her with this truth.

"That's right, Mom," I said, my voice hard. "The Hork-Bajir could die. Every single one of us, human and Hork-Bajir and Andalite, could die. Any day. At any time. I still don't get your point."

My mother gasped. It wasn't a fake gasp, either. She was shocked. "Cassie! How can you say that? We're talking about lives."

"I'm being realistic. This is a war, Mom. Do you understand what that means? Some of us are going to die. That's a fact. From disease or injury or deprivation. It doesn't much matter how, does it? Nothing we do now can change that fact. Not building a nicer shelter or being all pleasant to each other. Nothing will stop the dying except winning the war. And right now, our chances of winning don't look real good."

I turned from my mother's stricken face. Walked away.

Still angry at her for making me say the things I'd said.

Angry at myself because I knew I had hurt her.

Angry mostly because I had wanted to hurt her.

Because she was making me be the grown-up. And even after all the endless months of fighting, with all the disgusting acts I had witnessed — or committed — I still sometimes wanted to be normal again.

Also, because I was worried. Not just about my own parents.

If the adults didn't accept the reality of the war, they would never be prepared when the time came to fight.

And if they weren't prepared, they wouldn't survive.

# CHAPTER 4

M arco. Always vigilant. Always alert. Always scheming or, amazingly, figuring out the enemy's schemes.

I'd go spend some time with him. The one totally aware of our enormously serious situation.

Life is full of surprises.

Marco wasn't noodling with the design of the trenches. Or calculating a faster way out of the compound during an attack.

No. Marco was sitting on a stump, messing around with a stick and pocket knife. Like a guy with all the time in the world. Like a character on a rerun of *The Andy Griffith Show* on Nick at Nite.

"What are you doing?" I asked quietly.

He looked up at me and grinned.

"This, Cassie, is the almost-lost art of whittling. It's something people used to do when they were passing the time between milking the cows, plowing the back forty, and doing all kinds of labor-intensive jobs that are now rendered unnecessary by the proliferation of food courts."

"There's no food court around here," I pointed out. "And there's a lot of work to be done."

He smiled. He looked positively serene. This was not the Marco I knew.

"Yes, Cassie. There sure is a lot of work to be done. But didn't you see Jake give the go-ahead for a little downtime? All work and no play makes Marco one dull boy. So for once since this whole sorry mess began, I'm not worrying about what needs to be done."

"Where are your parents?" I said. "You could be helping them with something."

Yes, I sounded like a nag. A pain in the butt.

"My dad and mom are inside. They're figuring out how to mount a Dracon beam on the roof." He chuckled. "They're so romantic those two."

Marco's mother, Eva, was the former host body of the former Visser One. Long story short, we'd rescued the human and destroyed the Yeerk. Now Eva was back with her husband and son.

And Marco was thrilled. At least about his parents' reunion.

20

I tried to curb my mounting impatience. What was wrong with me? I mean, I was supposed to be the sensitive one. The one who understood people's feelings. The one who cared. The one who'd just walked away from Rachel for not considering Jake's feelings.

I should have been glad to see Marco so happy. Normally, I would have been. But so soon after the confrontation with my mother, Marco's good mood only annoyed me. Plucked my last nerve.

He was acting like my parents. Clearly, he was in denial.

And with Jake only partly focused on the mission, someone had to keep us in line.

"Marco, look," I said. "Downtime is one thing. But we can't just sit around. Sure, things seem peaceful. But the Yeerks are looking for us. Right now. As we speak."

He nodded. "Yep. I reckon you're right."

"Huh?"

All color drained from Marco's face. His voice was hushed. "I didn't really say that. Did I?"

I nodded.

Marco flipped the piece of wood over his shoulder, shut his knife with a snap, and stood.

"Okay. You're right. This R and R thing has got to stop. I could wind up dead. What do you want me to do? Build a catapult? Battering ram? Lead the Hork-Bajir in work songs?"

21

*"Galafth!"*

We froze.

Yeerks. So soon. We weren't ready! Not the Hork-Bajir. Not the Animorphs. And for sure not our parents.

Eva peeked out the door of the cabin, her expression tense. "We're powering up. You guys get out of the compound, spread out, and get ready to launch a counterattack."

Everywhere, Hork-Bajir and humans scrambled to take cover. I saw my parents standing off to the right. Frozen. Like they had no idea at all what they were supposed to do. I started toward them, but Marco grabbed the back of my shirt. "Let Toby handle it. You and I head for the trenches and . . ."

"Whoowhoo!"

The "all clear," a high-pitched whistle. The activity came to a halt.

"Was that a drill?" Marco wondered. "Maybe Jake and Toby set up a surprise . . ."

That's when I saw what had caused the disturbance. And I couldn't help but smile. The overall situation was as grim as it had been a moment ago, but my bad mood was lifting.

Two Hork-Bajir came into view. Between them marched Rachel's mom, Naomi. To say she looked mad was a huge understatement.

Rachel, Jake, and Ax emerged from the

trenches. Marco and I joined them at the center of camp.

The guards brought their prisoner to a halt before us.

"Mom." Rachel's voice was hard. She flung a clump of mud from her hand. "You tried to get away, didn't you? How many times do I have to tell you not to leave the camp?" She barked a very unhappy laugh. "Are you actually trying to get everybody killed?"

Rachel's mother yanked her arm from a Hork-Bajir's grasp.

"This is outrageous," she spit. "This is some kind of loony cult. Or a particularly weird and paranoid militia movement. If you don't let me contact the proper authorities, I'll —"

Rachel cut her off. "What authorities, Mom? The police, the FBI, and the CIA have all been infiltrated by Yeerks. So, who are you going to call? Your partner? He could be a Yeerk, too."

Naomi flinched.

"Rachel," Jake said quietly.

But Rachel wasn't ready to back off.

"This isn't one of your bogus lawsuits, Mom. This isn't something you can fix on paper. Okay? It's a *war*. We're not worrying about being sued. We're worried about being killed."

Rachel took a breath and continued. "Look, you're a lawyer. Maybe that's something back in your old life. But here it's useless and means nothing. But you can at least stay out of the way, follow orders, and try not to get us all killed."

Naomi's mouth trembled. I hoped she wouldn't cry. Watching an adult cry is one of the most unsettling, disturbing things a kid can see.

Okay, maybe Rachel's mother had deserved everything Rachel said. Yeah, she'd helped the Hork-Bajir write a constitution and was teaching some to read. But she'd also caused trouble for the camp with her general bad attitude. And her habit of sneaking away.

Still, I thought Rachel had gone way over the top.

I didn't condone her behavior, but I thought I understood it. Understood what had made Rachel go ballistic on her mom.

Like me, Rachel was scared.

# CHAPTER 5

**R**achel's sisters gathered protectively around their mother. Jordan took her hand. "I don't think you're useless, Mommy," she whispered.

A tear rolled down Sara's cheek.

Naomi swallowed hard and lifted her chin. Her eyes hardened and she looked at the two Hork-Bajir guards. "Don't touch me again," she said coldly. "Don't touch anyone in my family. If you do, I'll . . ." She broke off. Swallowed hard and tried again. "If you do I'll . . ."

Finally, the reality was dawning on her.

Rachel's tough-as-nails lawyer mother was realizing how incredibly vulnerable we all were.

I saw Marco smirk and turn away. His were

25

the only set of parents that had accepted their position as guerilla warriors — and as refugees.

Tears began to trickle down Naomi's face. It felt wrong to be watching her and doing nothing to help ease her pain. But would Naomi take comfort from her daughter's accomplice?

From a kid?

Then Eva joined the awkward group. Put her arm around Naomi's shoulders. "It takes a while to accept," she said softly. "Come on. Let's talk."

Slowly, the two women walked toward Eva's cabin. Jordan and Sara followed closely.

"Can you talk to Rachel?" I said quietly to Jake. "She explodes at her mom and it just makes Naomi more determined not to deal with this."

Jake's voice was impatient. "I've tried to talk to Rachel and she won't listen. So, no, I won't talk to her again. And no, I don't want to talk to you about my feelings."

I stood perfectly still, not trusting myself to move. I felt as if I'd been slapped.

Jake lowered his eyes, turned, and walked away.

I stalked after him. "Jake! Things are falling apart."

He whirled on me. His eyes were dark and wild. For the first time since I'd known and loved Jake, I was afraid of him. Afraid of what he might become.

"You think I don't know that?! I know we're

slipping up. Making mistakes. I know we're at one another's throats. And I know that if it weren't for Toby, this whole camp would probably be just a scar on the ground by now. What I don't know, Cassie, and this is the hard part . . . what I don't know is what I'm supposed to do about it."

I'd heard the expression, "my heart almost broke" before. Now, I knew what it meant.

I put my anger aside and fell into step beside Jake.

"It's going take time," I said calmly. "These people, our parents, have been dragged into this — into a refugee camp — against their wills. Their world has been torn apart. We have to respect their reluctance to fight alongside us. But, Jake, somebody's got to take charge."

"Fine. You do it."

"No," I said firmly. "I'm not a leader, Jake. You are. You're going to have to talk to my parents. And to Rachel's mother and sisters. Even Tobias's mom."

"Why should they listen to me?" Jake countered. "Look at the situation. We're hiding in the forest, living on the charity of the Hork-Bajir. If you were an adult — or even another kid, not Cassie — would you listen to me? No, you wouldn't. So why don't you just leave me alone?"

He looked at me. Then turned his head. "Please, Cassie."

Jake quickened his step and left me behind.

"Stop feeling sorry for yourself," I called after him. Desperate.

He didn't stop.

"You're acting like a coward!"

The moment the words were out of my mouth, I regretted them.

Jake stopped. Turned. His face was a stranger's. "*What* did you call me?"

He'd heard me. Too late to take back the words. "A coward," I repeated, flinching. "Now that it's the final crisis, you're turning chicken on us."

I didn't expect his weary laugh. "I'm not chicken," he said. "I'm just trying to give everybody a fighting chance. I'm not going to insist people do what I say when I don't have the slightest idea what's right or wrong. What's smart or stupid. Cassie, it's my fault we're on the run. You can't deny that."

I walked up to Jake, took a deep breath, and tried to sound reasonable. Reached for his hand and held it tight.

"Maybe you're right, Jake. And maybe you're wrong. Maybe you are a good leader, after all."

He tried to pull away but I wouldn't let him go.

"No, Jake. Listen. If that's the truth, you have to take charge. And if you really are a failure and it really is all your fault, then it's your responsibility to get us out of here. We need you, Jake. Either way, it has to be you."

It was a cheap shot. Jake's Achilles' heel has always been his sense of responsibility. I could see him weakening.

"Marco can be in charge," he said helplessly. Again he pulled his hand away. This time I let him go. "He's smarter than I am. Or Tobias. Or Ax. Or you. Rachel. Anyone. Anyone but me. You know why I was even in charge in the first place, Cassie? Because once upon a time, a long time ago, Marco said I was."

"Jake, that's not the whole truth . . ."

"Well, now my term of office is over," he continued bitterly. "So how about for once you guys figure things out and tell me what to do."

Then he turned and walked away.

And just kept walking.

# CHAPTER 6

That afternoon I lied and told everyone that Jake had called a meeting for later that evening.

Then I told Jake about the meeting. Two minutes before it was about to start.

He was not thrilled. But he wasn't angry, either. He was just . . . neutral.

Ever been to camp?

Sit around a fire with your friends?

Sing songs with your counselors? Roast marshmallows and tell scary stories?

Well, this wasn't like that at all. This was one sorry excuse for a camping experience.

The humans and Toby sat around a low fire covered with a damper. If we heard chopper blades overhead, the fire would be choked.

Every human face showed some level of fear. Tense with some level of uncertainty.

The Hork-Bajir were gathered just behind the circle of humans. Some sat, awkwardly. Others stood, towering.

Strangely enough, everyone was quiet. No bickering. No shrill whispering.

Jake stared into the fire.

Rachel folded her arms over her chest.

Marco stared up at the sky, like whatever was going on around the fire had nothing to do with him.

Ax hovered just behind Toby, his main eyes staring ahead. His stalk eyes scanning for trouble.

Loren and Tobias sat next to each other, shoulders touching. Tobias again in human morph. There, but somehow in a world of their own.

Toby peered across the fire. "Jake? You have called us together. Do you have something important to say?"

Jake looked up. Shook his head.

I stood. "Um. Actually. It was me. I called this meeting."

Rachel turned to me, curious. Marco and Tobias, too.

"I just wanted us all to talk," I explained. "Clear the air, if we can. We're not working together. Not as Animorphs. Not as families. Not as a camp."

No resistance so I went on.

"I know it's hard on you guys," I went on, looking at my parents, then at Rachel's mother. "But if you could just try to understand we're doing what we believe to be in everybody's best interest and . . ."

Rachel's mom let out a noise. A cross between "bah" and "harrumph."

I think it was lawyer talk for "cut the crap."

"Why am I being lectured to by you?" she demanded, looking at the other parents for support. "Why are we tolerating this? We're in the woods. We're living in filth — with aliens, for God's sake! And every time I try to leave — some creature, some fur-covered human abomination stops me. Let's face it."

Naomi looked at each adult in turn. "Michelle. Walter. Eva, Peter, Loren. We're being held prisoner. Why?"

Rachel leaned forward. Her eyes glittered dangerously.

"How many times do I have to say it, Mom? We're trying to stop the Yeerks from taking over the planet. And we're trying to stay alive while doing it. Trying to keep you alive, too. These past months, while you were busy fighting battles on paper and arguing in court, Jake and me and the others? We've been fighting."

Rachel's mother stood up. "I am sick to death of your insults. How did you turn out to be so arrogant? So sure nothing can be solved by compromise or negotiation. So sure all disagreements have to be settled by force or violence."

"That's our Rachel," Marco mumbled.

"Why won't you listen?!" Rachel cried.

Sara burst into loud sobs. "Mommy, I want to go home. I want Daddy!"

Naomi knelt and pulled her youngest child into her arms. Stroked the crying girl's head.

They weren't the only ones grieving for the safe, well-ordered life they had left behind.

There was a long silence, broken only by Sara's whimpering.

Finally, my dad spoke up.

"What do they want? These Yeerks. Cassie, surely they can be reasoned with; most people can be. What can we give them that would satisfy them?"

"Our souls," Jake answered quietly. The first words he had spoken all night. "If they don't already have them."

# CHAPTER 7

Jake stood. Reluctantly. But he stood.

"As long as Visser One is in charge, no negotiation is possible. He wants total control of Earth and everyone on it. If another visser comes into power, that might change. Maybe. But right now, we've got to deal with this reality."

"There are other vissers?" my dad asked hopefully. "Would it be possible to tell Visser One we'll negotiate, but not with him?"

Eva smiled slightly. Glanced at Jake, then back to my dad.

"I don't mean to sound condescending, Walter," she said. "But you have no idea who we're dealing with. If we approach Visser One for any reason, he'll kill us. Period. If we're lucky. If he stops to think, he'll probably torture us first. Just in case we've been holding back any useful information."

My mother shivered. My father put his arm around her shoulders.

Naomi looked at Rachel. Her face was tense. "I have three daughters to care for," she said. "A year from now, I want to still have three daughters. What do I have to do to keep them safe?"

"Believe that you're at war," Eva said simply. "You're a parent *and* a soldier. Learn to follow orders. Learn to respect experience."

"Okay, fine," Naomi answered crisply. "Eva, you used to be a big shot in the Yeerk organization. You know how the enemy thinks. What they're likely to do. And you're old enough to drive. I'll accept your word."

Eva shook her head. "There's only one enemy Visser One respects. And fears. And that's Jake. He needs to be our leader."

My father spoke up. "Even if he can do the job, he shouldn't be expected to. It's an enormous burden. It isn't fair to ask him."

*No one asked him in the first place,* I thought. *No one asked any of us.*

I looked at Jake. He looked like he was about to cry.

My father stood, walked to Jake's side, and put his hand on his shoulder. "I don't understand

35

all of this, Jake. I don't really know what happened to your parents. But until they come back . . . or . . . well, I want you to consider yourself part of our family."

Jake's mouth went tight. Yes, he was going to cry. I felt like I'd been punched in the stomach.

If Jake lost it, I'd lose it.

We'd all lose it. We'd all just break down into a sobbing, screaming, guilt-ridden, terrified group.

Kids. Adults. Hork-Bajir. Probably even Ax.

*Hold on.* I mentally willed Jake. *Hold on.*

I saw Rachel watching him, her blue eyes wide with concern. Even her mother, not Jake's biggest fan these days, seemed to be waiting for his reaction.

The Hork-Bajir watched Toby. They would take their cue from her. But Toby's eyes were glued on Jake. Her massive lower jaw jutted forward.

Jake was the center.

If the center didn't hold . . .

It seemed like we waited for hours. But it was probably only thirty or forty seconds before Jake stood taller and expelled his breath in a long, steady stream. He met my eyes, then my dad's. When he spoke, his voice was clear and strong.

"I appreciate that. I really do. And I appreciate the fact you don't think my being asked to lead is fair. The funny part is, I agree. It's not fair. But I guess it's no news that life's not fair."

Naomi mumbled something under her breath, then looked embarrassed for interrupting.

"Look," Jake went on. "This isn't the life I would have picked. Man, if I could go back, do it all over again . . . But I know that whether I like it or whether you like it, I'm the best-qualified person for the job. Understand me. I don't want it. I'm just saying I'm willing to do it. If you want me to. But it's your call."

My dad looked at my mom.

She turned to Eva.

Eva took her husband's hand. Nodded to Loren. Then, she raised her hand.

So did my mom.

So did my dad and Loren and Peter.

So did Toby and every Hork-Bajir.

Rachel's mom frowned. Looked around the group, from face to serious face. Finally, she raised her arm, only halfway, as if she were beaten.

"Mass psychosis," she pronounced. "That's all I can guess. So, what are your plans, Tsar Jake?"

"My plans?" Jake shoved his hands down into his pockets. "To keep us alive."

If this had been a movie, we all would have stood and cheered. Vowed to follow our leader anywhere, even to the grave. To die for the cause.

*Braveheart. The Patriot. Gladiator.* One for all. All for one.

Blah blah blah.

But it wasn't a movie. It was real.

I watched Jake's face. I had to admit he didn't exactly look like an inspirational leader.

He just looked like a sad, harried kid.

And it felt like my fault.

# CHAPTER 8

**E**arly the next morning, Jake called us together, privately.

"We can't go on like this," he said.

Marco choked on a laugh. "Now there's a profound statement."

Jake grinned wryly. "Let's review. Everything has changed. Our usual sources of information have pretty much dried up. The Chee are coming up with nothing, which means the Yeerks have tightened internal security."

"And the Yeerk resistance movement," I said. "We've lost touch with Mr. Tidwell at school. He's got to assume our disappearance means we've gone underground."

39

"So maybe we need to get in touch with him," Tobias suggested.

"Too slow," Rachel said. "We need action and results more than we need intelligence. Besides, for all we know Visser One has totally crushed the resistance."

<And now that we are in hiding,> Ax said, <it has become even more dangerous for me to attempt communication with the Andalite fleet commanders. The Yeerks are more determined than ever to locate the rebel force.>

Rachel frowned. "So, exactly what are we saying here?"

Jake looked at each of us in turn. "I think it's time," he said.

<You have come to a decision, Prince Jake?> Ax.

"Yes," he answered. "The morphing cube."

The morphing cube.

A gift.

And a curse.

There are times when we've been tempted to weight it down with bowling balls and drop it into the middle of the ocean.

The only problem is you still couldn't count on somebody not finding it someday.

"We can't go it alone anymore," Jake said. "The Yeerks know us. They know our names. They know our faces. If they take us down, there's nobody to replace us. The resistance is finished. It's time to build our forces. Reinforce our troops. The Chee can't help us here. The Yeerk resistance is a total unknown. And it's not like we can count on the Ellimist riding in to the rescue."

Marco scratched the back of his head like he was nervous. "More Animorphs? I just can't get comfortable with that."

"No way!" Rachel exploded. "We tried once. It was a disaster. Am I the only one who remembers David?"

No. She was not. I caught her eye then looked away.

Not long before, Rachel had encountered David again. A kid we'd deliberately made a *nothlit* after he attempted to give us up to the Yeerks.

A kid we'd reluctantly made an Animorph when his parents were taken and made Controllers.

From an average, if slightly troubled kid, to an Animorph, to spy and traitor. To rat. Forever.

Then, surprisingly, to tool of Crayak. The roughly equivalent, evil version of the Ellimist.

Long story short: Crayak hates Jake. He would do anything within the rules of his cosmic game to take Jake down. Recently, this involved pitting David against his ultimate enemy. Rachel.

In the end, Rachel had rejected Crayak's manipulations of her dark nature. Had refused to give up Jake. Had defeated David.

But had she killed David? I didn't know. She hadn't told me. She never would.

Marco nodded. "I'm with Rachel on this. No more Animorphs. Too big a risk."

"So maybe humans aren't the best choice for new Animorphs," Jake persisted. "What about the Hork-Bajir?"

There was a long pause. Then, as one, we all said, "No."

When you morph another animal, there's a short amount of time when the animal's brain, its instincts, pretty much dominates. It takes a lot of mental discipline and focus to get those animal instincts under control. To get them to work for, not against, your own brain.

The average Hork-Bajir probably couldn't handle that disturbing phase. Would succumb to the panic of the mouse or the aggression of the squid. Besides, Hork-Bajir didn't really need morphing ability, like we did. Their bodies were as well equipped for battle as any Earth creature they could morph.

"Okay, so it has to be people," Jake said. "What about the 'rents?"

"I'm overruled?" Marco said. "Okay, then. But not *my* parents." Marco's face was grim, not one trace of humor in his voice. "My mother's put in her time up front. And my dad's been through his own version of hell. He's officially dead, remember? Lost his job, his second wife . . ."

"What about Cassie's parents?" Jake asked. "Or Rachel's mother?"

Marco shook his head before I could say a word. "No offense, Cassie, but I think your parents may be bigger peace, love, hug-that-tree types than you are. If that's possible. And Rachel's mom is an even bigger loose cannon than Rachel."

"Hey!" Rachel barked.

"Okay! Okay!" Jake held up his hand. "We don't have time for this. Ticktock. We need ideas."

<Not my mother, either,> Tobias said. His hawk stare was more intense than usual. <Sorry. I can't deal. Okay, we've given her the morphing ability. And she'd probably fight if she had to. But after all she's been through . . . I mean, she doesn't even remember my father. Or me.>

"Not a problem," Jake assured him. "So, the parents are out of the running."

"It's got to be kids," Marco said musingly. "Adults are too reality-bound. It's too hard for them to suspend disbelief. Even when the new reality hits them in the face."

<Right.> Tobias. <Remember, we had some

43

degree of acceptance from those campers a while back. They thought we were cool. Okay, they also thought we were aliens, but still.>

"Yeah," Jake said. "We look for other kids. But we still have a problem. 'Cause we're gonna have to figure out who's a Controller and who's not. Every day, every hour, counts. And we don't have time to watch our recruits for three days before we make a move."

Fact: Controllers have to return to a Yeerk pool every three days to feed on Kandrona rays. If they don't, they're facing starvation. A horrible way to die by anyone's standards.

Unfortunately, about the only way to be completely sure people don't have a Yeerk snuggled somewhere in their cranial cavities is to watch them for three days. If they make no attempt to find a Kandrona source, you know they're okay.

<There's got to be another way,> Tobias challenged. Then, excitedly, <What's the one sort of person the Yeerks won't touch? Who do we know for sure isn't one of them?>

It took me a minute.

Then, I got it.

44

# CHAPTER 9

"The Yeerks don't infest people like your mom was before she could morph," I said honestly. "The Yeerks don't want a blind Controller. They don't want a disabled Controller. Deaf people, people in wheelchairs, people with serious illnesses."

"She's right," Rachel said slowly. "I've never seen a Controller in a wheelchair. And I bet any human-Controller who gets cancer or loses a limb is killed. No joke."

<Hundreds, thousands of people,> Tobias said. <The Yeerks just write them off. So do a lot of humans.>

"So do a lot of aliens," Marco added, giving Ax a look.

<It makes sense that the Yeerks would not re-
cruit the permanently sick or injured. Those
people are defective. *Vecols.* They would not be
useful in a battle,> Ax responded coldly.

"Not every species measures an individual's
worth by the ability to fight," I said.

Ax nodded. "I understand. But the Yeerks do
not."

Marco laughed. "If a guy in a wheelchair could
morph a grizzly, he could fight. He could kick
some serious butt."

Rachel frowned. "The thing is, morphing will
only restore you to the way you were born, right,
Ax?"

Ax nodded and Rachel continued, "One of
the disabled kids might miss the two-hour time
limit. Let's say someone with only one leg. She
might have to demorph in the middle of a battle.
And she'd be helpless to save herself. To get
away."

"No more helpless than we've often been in
that kind of situation," Jake said thoughtfully.

Before I could stop it, the air seemed to leave
my lungs. How could we live with ourselves if one
of the new and very inexperienced Animorphs got
seriously injured in battle? Died, even? There
was something wrong with the whole idea.

"We're not doing this," I said quietly but with
conviction.

<It was your idea,> Tobias pointed out gently.

"No," I protested. "I was just thinking out loud. I wasn't suggesting we actually do it. It's not right."

Jake cleared his throat. "Cassie, recruiting handicapped kids, or differently abled kids, or whatever we should say, might be our only chance of survival."

"Our chance of survival. What about theirs? We're going to use kids less fortunate than us to keep us alive? Why are we so important? Why are we more important than anyone else?"

"That's not what we're saying, Cassie." Jake's voice was low but firm. "Handicapped people live on this planet, too. When I say 'our' chance of survival, I'm including every human being on Earth. Everyone has a stake in this fight. Why not give other kids the power they need to fight back?"

I didn't know what to say. Jake was right.

Suddenly, a revelation. I was thinking like my mother. She was right about the emergency living conditions the Hork-Bajir had built.

Still, she couldn't get over thinking her job was to take care of the Hork-Bajir. It wasn't. Her job was only to help the Hork-Bajir help themselves.

Would we be doing the same by giving handicapped kids the power to morph? Helping them to help themselves? Arming them to defend their homes, their families, their worlds?

47

Or would we just be burdening them with an unendurable load of misery, guilt, and pain?

"It's not like we'd force anyone to accept the technology," Rachel murmured. "It would be every kid's choice."

Marco nodded. Like he was convincing himself the scheme was a good thing. The right thing.

"Tell them what's going down," he said. "Offer them a way to fight back. To resist. If they don't want to get involved, fine. All right, more Animorphs means more of a security risk, but at this point, I'm not sure that's such a big deal."

"Wait a minute," I said. "There's something else. Look at what happened with Loren. She was blinded in an accident. Tobias gave her the ability to morph, and now she's not blind. Like Rachel and Ax said, morphing repairs DNA."

<But wait — it *didn't* give her back her memory,> Tobias pointed out. <She still has amnesia.>

"That's my point," I pressed. "We don't know exactly how morphing works in every situation. With each individual."

<There is no uncertainty in Andalite morphing technology,> Ax said firmly.

"Maybe not for Andalites," I argued. "Though we know some Andalites are allergic to the technology. Remember Mertil. But maybe there's uncertainty for humans. We just don't know. No

48

one's done studies. And our doctors don't know everything there is to know about the causes of human diseases."

"Conclusion?" Rachel asked.

"That some of the kids we give the morphing technology to might be cured. And then what? Then where do they go? How can you ask someone who can walk for the first time in years to pretend she can't? To stay in a hospital? I mean, the Yeerks notice someone who could only get around in a wheelchair is suddenly running marathons, the person's cover is blown. She's taken, infested, gives up everyone else. Or else she's forced to disappear."

"Cassie's got something there, Jake," Marco said. "From a practical standpoint we don't need more refugee Animorphs. We need soldiers we can trust to stay undercover for as long as possible. Can we count on a kid who's suddenly healthy to give up his newfound freedom for the sake of a mission that sounds like a *Star Trek* plot? I'm just saying there's a major trust issue here."

Jake nodded. "Okay. So this idea isn't clean. It's risky. Maybe even morally suspect." He looked at me. "If you want to think about it. But I don't think we have that kind of time anymore. I say we do it. Marco?"

Marco hesitated then nodded.

"Tobias? Rachel?"

"I'm in."

<I'm in, too.>

"Ax?"

<Yes. I am also in.>

Jake grinned. For a minute he seemed like the old Jake again. Full of energy and confidence.

That should have made me happy. But it didn't.

Because I didn't like what we were about to do. And because it was clear that in this situation, Jake didn't care what I thought.

Jake and I are closer than just friends. We care a lot about each other.

Or at least we used to.

Now everything was changing. Everybody was changing. I didn't know who was who anymore. Sometimes, I didn't even know what I felt.

"Ax, Marco, get on the Web," Jake said. "Find us a way to reach some likely candidates. Remember, they have to be kids. Locate a clinic. A physical rehab hospital. Whatever."

Jake looked to Rachel and Tobias. "Just be ready, you two. Keep an eye on the parents. And don't let them get wind of our plan. I'm betting it would seriously freak them out."

"We're on it, fearless leader." Marco.

The fire of determination — of possibility — burned in Jake's eyes. "We'll start out with a small test group. If it works, we'll expand. And if we can expand enough, we'll have Yeerks chasing Animorphs everywhere."

The others scattered, hurrying to carry out orders.

Finally, Jake looked at me. Some of the old, inspirational Jake in his expression.

"Cassie? You're with us, right?"

I was angry. And I was hurt.

But what could I do?

I'd been the one to insist we follow Jake.

My Jake.

How could I refuse now?

# CHAPTER 10

Marco had a lead. A rehab center for kids in a town not too far away.

We decided that Jake, Marco, and I would go. It was too dangerous for all of us to travel together now that the Yeerks knew who we were. And someone needed to stay at camp in case of a surprise Yeerk attack — to look after the parents in case we didn't make it back.

We traveled in our bird-of-prey morphs, together but apart. Jake, as peregrine falcon. Marco and I, osprey. Ax had broken down the morphing cube so that each of us could carry a small piece.

One problem. Jake had suggested that we not

fly directly to the rehab center. That we make a detour, in case we were being watched.

It made sense. But I couldn't understand why Jake insisted on such a roundabout — and dangerous — path. When Marco challenged the idea — "You're joking, right, dude?" — Jake reacted with anger.

"You agreed to the plan. So we do it my way. End of story."

Marco is Jake's best friend. He's also very smart. He knows how to pick his battles.

"Hey, sorry, you're right. Your wish is my command."

And then he looked at me and I knew he'd be on extra high alert.

We landed and demorphed in an alley behind a bicycle shop only a few blocks from the rehab center.

Over time we'd learned to morph slightly more clothing than too-small spandex. In this instance, a few pieces of ratty cycling gear was exactly right. Three kids in bike shorts hanging around outside a bicycle shop means squat. Okay, we still hadn't learned to morph shoes but . . .

At least twenty bicycles — mountain bikes, road bikes, and hybrids — were parked against a long rack on the sidewalk in front of the shop.

Some weren't locked. Helmets hung from the handlebars of about ten of the bikes.

"So, Jake. Let me get this straight." Marco. "We snag three bikes and ride over to the rehab center." And then, as if to convince himself: "Okay. Nobody will pay any attention to us. Everyone rides bikes."

Jake nodded. "We hide in plain sight."

"Getting back to the bikes," I said. "By 'snag,' I assume you mean 'steal.'"

Marco rolled his eyes. "Semantics. I prefer to use the word 'borrow.' We'll try to return the bikes as soon as possible."

Jake glanced up and down the street. "This is it," he said.

I couldn't help myself. I protested, again. "Jake . . ."

Jake shot me a look. It wasn't a friendly one.

I was stung. I looked away.

"I've never stolen a bike," Jake said to Marco. "Any suggestions?"

Marco pretended to look hurt. "What makes you think I know how to steal a bike? However, I would suggest we, er, just pick three unlocked bikes and casually ride away."

"What if somebody comes out of the shop and sees us?" I asked.

"Pull a Lance Armstrong. Smoke them. Ride

away really, really fast." Marco strode forward and removed a red road bike from the rack.

We were out in the open. Vulnerable. I'd been in a hundred horrible battles with a mind-boggling array of aliens. But I swear, my heart was beating faster now than it ever had when I was in morph, facing down battalions of inter-galactic monsters.

Just as I was slinging my leg over the bar of a black hybrid, I heard it.

"Andalites! Rebels!"

Tseeeew! Tseeeew!

Three human-Controllers came bursting out of the bicycle shop. Dracon beams singed my hair.

Of course the Yeerks would have every inch of every local town covered. The one bicycle shop, the three Starbucks, the massive Barnes & Noble, the four McDonald's. Of course they would be waiting for us.

Why had Jake insisted on this obviously dangerous scheme? Why had Marco and I catered to his need for — what? Danger? An adrenaline rush?

For a split second I thought the impossible.

That Jake really had lost his ability to think clearly as a leader. That by pushing him so hard I'd sent him careening over the edge.

Not the time for contemplation.

"Let's go!" he yelled.

We were off!

Wham! WhamWhamWham! The slam of car doors. The Controllers were going to follow us by car. They would overtake us in seconds.

"Get off the street!" Jake ordered. He bumped up the curb onto the sidewalk. Tore into an alley too narrow for a car to follow.

Marco and I followed him, pedaling furiously.

The alley was only about twenty feet wide. We raced past overflowing garbage cans, a sleeping cat, an abandoned couch. Bumped over crumbled concrete, broken glass, and an empty can of gasoline. Rode like crazy until the alley came to a dead end.

Now what?

Slapslapslapslap!

Footsteps ringing on the pavement behind us! The human-Controllers were on foot now. Getting closer.

"Morph," Jake ordered.

"Battle morphs?" Marco dropped his bike with a clatter.

"No." Jake nodded toward one of several doors that led from the alley into the various shops that faced the street. "Roach."

This time, the morph started almost before I got the full picture of a roach in my mind.

WHOOSH!

I shrank to the dirty ground.

SCHLOOP!

A mini-Cassie. Small enough so that a shard of glass seemed like a boulder.

At the speed of a fast-forwarded videotape, the roach's exoskeleton covered my body.

The body segmented. Sprouted antennae and all the other nasty parts that made the roach nearly invincible.

The morph was done almost before it had started.

All around me, I felt the vibration of the Controllers' pounding feet. Too late. We slipped through a crack beneath a doorway and disappeared.

Demorphed and surveyed the area.

The space was dark and dusty. I fought the urge to sneeze.

Voices and light came from an adjoining room. The door was partly opened. Jake motioned for silence. We peered around the open door.

And saw an elderly lady holding a big sword.

"Now this is very popular," she told a group of kids about our age. Maybe a bit older. "Pirates are very big right now."

I stepped back, turned, and found myself face-to-face with a pale woman with long red hair. I almost screamed, then caught myself.

Not a person. A wig on a styrofoam head.

Marco pulled an obviously fake rabbit out of a top hat.

Jake reached for a Spider-Man mask.

We were in the storeroom of a costume shop.

# CHAPTER 11

"I feel stupid."

"You look stupid," I confirmed.

Marco's magician's outfit was seriously cheesy. A shiny polyester jumpsuit that was supposed to look like a tux. It looked more like a Las Vegas showgirl's outfit, complete with voluminous gold lamé cape.

I looked pretty stupid myself, dressed up like a fortune-teller from a classic B-movie.

"Sssh!"

The bangles would have to go, I realized. Too much noise.

"Sorry," I whispered to Jake. I slipped off the cheap jewelry and placed it on a shelf.

Marco grunted. "How come he's the only one who doesn't look like a total fool?"

It was true. The only costume Jake could find that fit him at all decently was modeled on that of a 1950s' Beat poet or something. Black turtleneck, black jeans, black shoes, a black beret. Even a phony goatee.

"Soul patch, I think," Marco corrected.

I volunteered to carry the reassembled morphing cube in one of the interior pockets of my many-layered skirt.

We'd come up with a plan. As always, it was risky. But we didn't have a lot of choice: We could go back into the alley as roaches and get crushed under the heels of waiting human-Controllers. We could walk out into the alley as humans and be captured. Or, we could storm out in battle morphs, be forced to fight, and maybe never make it to the rehab center.

Our immediate mission was clear. Locate more potential Animorphs. Get home alive.

So we slipped out of the storeroom and fell in with the group of about fifteen variously costumed kids as they left the shop.

They called themselves the "Revelers." They were students at a local magnet school for the performing arts. And they were on their way to put on a show for the kids at the rehab center.

It was almost too good to be true.

Marco made a few remarks about guys in tights.

Jake reacted like the old Jake. Afraid there might be Yeerks in the group.

A reasonable concern, given recent events. Controllers seemed to be everywhere. But Yeerks on a recruiting mission wouldn't be headed to a place that housed sick and disabled humans. I hoped.

The rehab center adjoined a large hospital complex. I counted sixteen floors aboveground.

We followed at the back of the troop of entertainers. Right through the front door, past the nurse at the admissions desk and the guards roaming the lobby.

No one questioned us.

Finally, we reached a ward at the back of the ground floor.

The ward was full of little kids.

The oldest was maybe seven. Some were in wheelchairs. Some wore casts. Some were in hospital beds.

Even so, you could still feel all that wiggly, giggly little-kid energy.

The kids squealed and laughed and applauded as we entered.

The troop launched right into some hokey song about sunshine and flowers, smiles and showers. They'd choreographed a simple dance for the song. Simple if you were a dance major at a school for the performing arts.

Marco gave me his exaggerated panicked look.

"Stay in the back," I mouthed.

"Sneak out," Jake added.

"Sunshine is just fine all the time!" sang the Revelers.

And as the group began to step-step-step to the left, I step-step-stepped right. Out the door and into the hall.

A few steps later, Marco and Jake joined me.

Jake glanced back the way we'd come.

"No good," he said. "These kids are too little."

"The older kids might be on another floor," Marco said.

"Okay. We go from floor to floor until we find them. Keep up the entertainment act."

I laughed. "Yeah, that'll be easy."

Marco spread open his gold lamé cape. "Easier than you think," he said. *"Voilà!"* He reached inside and pulled out a pigeon. A live pigeon.

"Where did you get that?" Jake hissed.

Marco smiled. "It was on the sidewalk. Something's wrong with its wing. But it doesn't seem to be in pain. I figured if we recruit anybody today, they'll need a morph that will get them out of here without attracting attention."

Gently, Marco replaced the pigeon back in his cape.

Jake's face froze. I knew what was going through his mind. Knew he was beating himself for not having thought of this contingency. For the fiasco outside the bike shop.

"What?" Marco pouted. "You've got something better? Maybe a fluffy bunny?"

"Maybe we should just get out of here," Jake said tightly. "I'm getting a bad feeling about this. I don't . . . We'll try again tomorrow."

A harried nurse came striding toward us, shoes squeaking on the polished floor. She smiled and continued on. Clearly, a bunch of kids in costume were not her priority.

When she had passed, Marco frowned. "Jake, I've been hanging in there until now. But I'm going to fight you on this one. After what happened earlier, this may be our last chance to get in here without basically advertising our plan to the Yeerks. Or making this staff suspicious. I say we take the chance, finish the job. Now."

Marco was right.

I scooped up an armload of magazines from a table next to a lumpy couch. Distributed them among the three of us. "Here," I said. "Follow me."

We got to a bank of elevators. I pushed the

button. The doors opened with a *ding!* and we stepped inside. A doctor looked up from a clipboard and gave us an amused smile. I smiled back brightly. And for a moment wondered if I were staring at a Yeerk.

We rode in silence until the door opened at the third floor. The doctor stepped forward and, before leaving the elevator, spoke. "Look in on the fifth floor if you have time. Some of those kids are about your age. They could use some company."

"Okay," I said, still smiling.

The door began to close and Marco pushed the button for the fifth floor.

Jake put his hand against the elevator door to keep it from closing. "Maybe he's setting us up."

I took Jake's hand from the door and let it close. "You're right, Jake. It could be a trap. We've walked into them before. Let's try to deal with this and try not to choke. Okay?"

"Are you patronzing me?" he asked, unbelievingly.

"Yeah, Jake. I am."

Marco pushed the button again and smiled bleakly. "Take it from me, Jake-meister. You get used to it after a while."

# CHAPTER 12

The door opened on the fifth floor. At one end of the hall, just before a set of double doors, was a sort of communal area. Several severely disabled kids sat in wheelchairs, watching TV and playing cards. The rest of the hall was empty.

Those who could, looked over to see who was coming.

No wiggly, giggly excitement here.

Basically, the mood was pretty down.

But the kids were about our age. That was something.

We glanced uncertainly at one another. Then I stepped ahead and led Jake and Marco toward the group at the end of the hall. "Hi!" I said brightly. "Anybody want a magazine?"

One boy, almost completely immobilized, pressed his right finger against the switch on his power chair and scooted away without a word.

His rejection shouldn't have hurt but it did.

Two girls in wheelchairs were playing cards at a small table.

"Did I say something wrong?" I asked them.

One of the card players, a pale girl with short blonde hair, gave me a cool look and lifted her brows disdainfully.

"No. He's just afraid you guys are going to sing."

The other cardplayer at the table laughed. She was wearing an Olympics T-shirt and sweats with a NIKE logo printed down the outside of the right leg.

"Sorry," Marco said. "I left my harmonica at home. But I can do magic tricks. Sort of."

The pale girl looked at Marco steadily. "I've seen David Copperfield in New York. Siegfried and Roy in Las Vegas. And Penn and Teller in Los Angeles. You really think I want to see your act?"

Then she turned her attention back to the cards.

The girl in the sweats smiled. "Come on," she said. "He may not be a pro, but everybody deserves a shot."

"Yeah and some people deserve to be shot," the cold girl snapped.

We were getting nowhere with this entertainment approach. And we were getting there fast.

"Okay," Marco muttered. "Remind me again why we're here?" Then he turned to an Asian boy sitting in a wheelchair to the right of the blonde girl. "What about you? Can I interest you in a few one-hundred-percent-guaranteed-to-fail amateur magic tricks?"

I'd seen the boy's head bobbing slightly as he divided his attention between the card game and the TV. I guessed he had cerebral palsy.

Now his face contorted and his body stiffened with effort. "D . . . d . . . d . . ."

The pale girl with the cards calmly and patiently rearranged her hand. And waited.

The boy's attempts to speak were painful to witness.

"Dii . . . diii . . . diiiii . . ."

Jake and Marco looked panicked. Confused. I guess I did, too. What were we supposed to do now? Wait for the boy to finish? Leave? Pretend we didn't realize he was trying to say something?

I looked to the blonde girl for help. She lifted her eyebrows. Okay. It was clear she expected us to finish what we had started.

The Asian boy took a last shuddering breath and expelled a word. Just one word, but he expelled it triumphantly.

"DITTO!"

The pale girl burst into laughter. The boy giggled. Both were delighted with their own rudeness.

"He was supposed to have it an hour ago. He's in pain."

I turned toward the sound of the voice. It was young but mature. And angry.

And it belonged to another kid in a wheelchair. I noticed he had nice hair. Kind of gold-brown and wavy.

"How do you know he's in pain?" a male nurse argued.

"It's his eyes. If you'd take the time to look, his eyes will tell you a lot."

"James, I know you're Pedro's roommate, but . . ."

"I'm not just his roommate," the kid — James — snapped. "I'm his friend. And since he can't talk to you, I'm doing it for him. If you guys can't get the medication here on time, just leave it on his night table. I'll give it to him."

The pale girl backed her wheelchair away from the table. "I'll be back," she told the other two.

We followed her partway down the hall, uninvited.

"Look," the nurse said. "We're short-staffed. I'm sorry Pedro had to wait, but we can't let you give him his medication. You're not authorized."

"I've been here longer than you have," James retorted. "I've been here longer than anybody," he added dryly. "I would think that gives me some rights."

The nurse hesitated a second, then reluctantly nodded. "Okay. Okay. I'll get it right now." He hurried away.

The girl wheeled up beside James and spoke quietly.

James looked around and saw us hovering. "Well?" he said angrily. "Who's the show here? Us or you?"

# CHAPTER 13

Marco swept his cape in a glittering arc. "We are," he said quickly.

James and the girl gave him a long, level stare.

"My infamous charm doesn't seem to work in this place," Marco said under his breath.

Then there was a sound from the room behind James.

"See you later," James said. The pale blonde girl nodded and wheeled back toward us.

James turned abruptly and wheeled into the room. Again, we followed.

A boy lay on the bed closest to the door. His dark hair had been badly cut, at places way too

70

close to his head. His eyes followed James closely. The rest of him was still.

James wheeled himself over to the boy's bedside. "The nurse is coming with your medicine, Pedro. Don't worry. It'll be here soon. You want to hear some music?"

Pedro's eyes closed then opened.

"Rock?"

Pedro stared, unblinking.

"Country western?"

Pedro's eyes flickered, the lashes fluttered.

"Country western it is," James said, wheeling himself over to the radio. "Though I don't understand how you can listen to that stuff, man," he teased. "Sure I can't talk you into some Blink 182?"

We backed away from the door.

"What now?" Jake whispered. "How are we going to get through to these kids?"

"We're not." Marco. "They hate us."

"Sorry about the rude reception." It was the girl in the sweats. "I'm Collette."

"Hi. I'm Cassie. This is Marco. And this is Jake. We came to entertain but, um, we seem to be going about it the wrong way."

"Yeah," Marco added. "The little kids seemed glad to see us. What's with the big attitude up here?"

Collette began to wheel back toward the group. We walked beside her.

"Let me tell you something," she said. There was no anger or bitterness in her voice. "A disabled kid is like the kitten who becomes a cat. You're a kitten, everybody wants to pet you and play with you. You get a little older, you're just a nuisance. Some of the people here haven't been home in years."

She pointed back toward James's room. "About all he has to look forward to is a nursing home when he's too old for this place. And he's been here since he was a little kid. He got hit by a drunk driver when he was four. His mother brought him in to be operated on and never came back to get him."

"Okay." Marco. "He can have all the attitude he wants."

Jake cleared his throat. I heard what Jake had heard. James, coming out of his room. He wheeled past us and on down the hall.

"Where's he going?" I asked.

"There's another lounge further down the hall. Through those double doors. It's a good place to go if you want some privacy. The door shuts. James spends a lot of time there."

"Think we could talk to him?" I asked.

"You could try," Collette answered. "James isn't too friendly. But he's cool. He's the one who makes sure we get what we need. He's the man. Even the nurses and doctors listen to what he says."

"A leader," Jake said.

"Yeah. He's gone to bat for me a couple of times. Not that I really need much help," Collette added quickly. "I've got family and stuff."

"So, how come you're not giving us the cold shoulder?" Marco asked.

She patted the sides of her chair. "This is just a temporary thing for me. I'm not usually in a chair. I had a skiing accident and this place has the best pediatric orthopedic staff around. I came in for some surgery on my knees. Any of you guys ski?"

"Once," Marco answered. "Didn't like it. Too cold. And chicks don't dig it when you fall, like, every three seconds."

Collette made a face like Marco was nuts. "Oh man. You're missing the greatest sport there is. Maybe you're more into skating? I like skating but it's a little tame for me. I'm into the extreme, high-risk stuff."

"Collette!" At the end of the hall the pale girl beckoned. "You want to play cards or not?"

Collette put her hands on her wheels. "I need to get back. That's Kelly. She's got cystic fibrosis. It makes her so weak sometimes, she can barely shuffle the cards. We play a lot when she feels strong. The other guy is Timmy," she added. "Stop by before you go." Collette winked at Marco. "I like company."

"If she's only recently injured, it's possible she's a Controller," Jake said as Collette rejoined Kelly.

"True," Marco answered with a grin. "But I don't know. She's just too cute. Did you see that? She winked at me!"

"Don't get attached," Jake said tiredly. "Life is probably going to be a lot shorter than you thought it would be."

Marco's grin faded. "You know what, Jake? You don't have to remind me about that."

For about a split second, Jake looked embarrassed. "Sorry," he mumbled.

"It's okay, dude. It gets to us all."

"Come on," Jake said quickly. "Let's find James."

# CHAPTER 14

James's expression never changed.

Not once.

Not when Jake told him that aliens called Yeerks had invaded the planet.

Not when Jake told him about finding the crashed spaceship.

Not when Jake told him about Elfangor, the Andalites, and the morphing cube.

Not when Jake told him about how Visser One, then Visser Three, had killed Elfangor and eaten him.

Just continued to watch Jake with an unblinking stare. Completely unmoved. Supremely unimpressed.

He didn't even change expression when Jake

told him we were looking for a few good Animorphs.

When Jake finished, there was a long, long silence.

Finally, James looked away from Jake to Marco. Then to me. Then he sighed heavily, bored and contemptuous.

"I'm sure when you talked about this at school, it seemed like a really good joke. But when you go back, you can give your friends a message from the 'gang-of-pathetically-grateful-for-attention-kids-at-the-rehab-center.'"

"But . . ." I began.

He cut me off. His voice was more than sarcastic.

"You can tell your idiotic little friends that yeah, we have our problems. But at least we don't get our kicks by dressing up like refugees from a fifth-rate school play and playing tricks on people in wheelchairs."

"You know what?" Jake said, with a bitter laugh. "I don't need this. I'm telling you the truth. You can believe me or not. It's your funeral."

James's face went red. He started to wheel himself out of the room but Jake grabbed his arm. "Wait!"

Marco and I stepped back. Stunned by Jake's harsh words.

James wrenched his arm out of Jake's grasp.

"Don't touch me, man," he warned. "I may be in a chair but I can kick your butt if I have to."

Jake reached for James again. With a lightning quick motion, James grabbed Jake's other arm, angled his chair so that it caught Jake behind the ankle, and flipped him to the ground.

"Umpff!"

Had I used the word *helpless* in describing kids like James?

James looked down at Jake and cocked an eyebrow. "You don't even want to know what Kelly can do to you, you make her mad enough."

Jake lay sprawled on the floor, like a guy who'd just had a bucket of cold water dumped on him.

He started to climb to his feet. "Look . . ." Then he stopped and shook his head. "Demonstration time."

Marco crossed his arms. "Go for it, dude. We've got nothing left to lose."

Jake closed his eyes.

Watching Jake morph while standing next to somebody who had never seen the process was a little like watching it for the first time.

It was horrible, ugly, grotesque, and fascinating all at once.

First, Jake's throat bulged out like he'd swallowed an orange. Whole. Then huge cords in his neck knotted and stretched as if something alive were trapped in his throat.

Then, in one swift movement, his human face was remolded into that of a powerful feline. Human features reimagined.

I looked down at James.

He didn't seem afraid. Just alarmed. Concerned.

He wheeled a few feet backward. "Calm down, man," he mumbled. "Just take it easy."

Jake's legs shortened and bent at a seemingly impossible angle.

"I'll get a doctor." James turned his chair sharply toward the door.

"No!" Marco grabbed the handles of James's chair and turned him back to face Jake.

POP! POP!

Jake's eyes bulged and gleamed like yellow marbles. The sockets pouched out and flattened. The bridge of his nose and his cheeks melded together. Tufts of black-and-orange fur appeared randomly, then sprouted faster and faster in a striped blur.

Two and a half seconds later the morph was complete.

There we were. A gypsy. A magician. A kid in a wheelchair. And a tiger.

"I think I took the wrong medication," James gasped. "I'm seeing things. Actually, why don't you guys get a doctor? For me."

The door opened and we heard a gasp.

"Amazing!"

James whirled around. Collette sat in the doorway, her mouth open. "Allow me to apologize on Kelly's behalf. I don't think even Siegfried and Roy could sneak a tiger by the front desk at this place."

James blinked. "You see it, too?"

Collette wasn't listening. She wheeled slightly closer to Jake. "Is he totally tame? Can I pet him? Wow! I'm so impressed. I'm going to get the others."

"Hold it!" James maneuvered his chair so that it blocked her exit.

"What?"

<If she goes out and tells people there's a tiger on the floor, any human-Controllers on staff will know right away we're here.>

Collette was startled. "Who said that?"

James pointed at Jake. "He did," he answered weakly.

"You're a ventriloquist?" Collette asked Marco.

Marco took a deep breath. "We'd better go through this one more time."

# CHAPTER 15

What can I say?

Some people suspend disbelief with no trouble at all. Collette was one of them.

First, I explained about Jake. That he was the tiger. I explained about morphing. That it was possible. And that we were looking for more Animorphs.

"We could do this?" Collette gasped. "I could do this?"

Jake, back to his human self, nodded.

"Are you kidding? How do I learn? When can I start?"

"Hold it," James barked. "You haven't heard the whole story. This isn't just some kind of vir-

tual reality ride. It's about . . . I can't explain it,"
he admitted. "You tell her."

So Jake told Collette about the Yeerks.

Collette's eye's widened. "So, like, it's dangerous? Morphing?"

"Very," Marco confirmed. "It's not something
we do for fun. Well, most times. It's a weapon.
Personally, I hate the danger part," he con-
fessed. "But you're into the whole reckless behavior thing, right? Extreme sports, bungy
jumping, alligator wrestling."

Collette looked embarrassed and didn't answer.

"Why us?" James asked abruptly. "There are
thousands of kids who would sign on for a mission like this. Maybe millions. Kids with macho
fantasies. Kids with healthy legs. Healthy lungs.
Kids with something to prove. Kids who can run
and jump. Kids who don't need help going to the
bathroom."

How did you tell people that even aliens from
outer space considered them "defective"?

"Because the Yeerks are jerks," I blurted.

Jake and Marco smiled. Jerks. Major understatement. But true.

"They don't want your bodies as hosts."

"Are you saying we're useless?" James's voice
had a dangerous edge. His blue eyes darkened.

"Not to us," Jake said quickly. "That's why we're here."

"So what do you want from me? Specifically?" he asked.

"I want you to help us. You seem to be the leader around here. The other kids here will listen to you before they listen to me. Talk to some of them. At least three or four to start."

James shook his head. "No. It's one thing to do something risky myself. To make that choice. It's another thing to ask others to put their lives on the line for a cause that might or might not even be real."

"It's real," Marco said.

James shook his head. "Doesn't matter. I don't want the responsibility of somebody getting hurt — or dying — because of me. You may think our lives don't mean much to us, because they don't mean much to other people. But we do value our lives. And one another."

I knew James meant every word.

"Come on, Collette." James turned to go, then wheeled back to face us. "Don't worry about us talking. I won't. And if Collette does, well . . . just don't worry about that."

"Won't you even talk to some of the others?" Marco pleaded.

"No," James answered flatly.

"Look," I said. "You started out angry. You thought we were playing with your head, dissing you because you're in a wheelchair. But don't you see? That's exactly what you're doing to the others. To your friends."

"What?" James snapped.

"Acting like they're babies," I said.

Hardly believing it was me talking.

"Or dumb. Like they're not capable of giving informed consent. Look, James." I knelt by his side so that I was looking up at his face. "I know this whole story about the Yeerks is hard to believe, but you have to believe. Your friends' lives are already at stake. You need to have some means of protecting yourselves if the Yeerks get any stronger. Look, they might not want to infest you. But they will want to kill you."

The words came without interruption. But inside, my conscience was rebelling at every syllable. I was trying to convince James to be a recruit, to recruit others to our cause. Me, the one who'd been against the plan from the beginning.

But being here, talking to James, seeing these kids, I realized in a serious way, maybe for the first time, that they weren't helpless.

Just like our parents.

"You know what," I continued. "You don't really have a choice here. This is duty time.

You've been tapped. So step up to the plate. Whatever. Fact is, we need you. Your friends need you."

Marco and Jake looked at me with raised eyebrows.

James was silent.

Finally, he looked at Jake through narrowed eyes. Jake stared back. Neither one was going to look away.

"I've got two conditions," James said slowly.

"Yeah?"

"One. I pick my own team. You may not approve of the choices. But if it's my team I pick its members. I'm responsible for them."

Jake nodded. "Fine."

"Two. No matter what happens, I want Pedro to acquire a morph. A good one. He's been in that bed his entire life. Fourteen years, flat on his back. Even if I don't make it out alive, I want Pedro to have at least two hours of freedom."

Jake nodded. "We can do that."

James held out his hand.

Jake shook it.

# CHAPTER 16

James assembled Collette, Timmy, and Kelly. Marco stood guard at the door to the small lounge.

Collette had suspended disbelief pretty easily.

But Timmy and Kelly were the ultimate "show me" freaks.

First, Jake told them about the Yeerks. Collette and James confirmed they'd been told the same information. Timmy and Kelly were still dubious.

So Jake, Marco, and I had to go through a large part of our repertoire of morphs before they were convinced morphing wasn't some kind of cheap parlor trick. No smoke and mirrors. No ghostly projections.

Once they believed, they were excited. Very excited.

"This is our way out of here for good," Kelly gasped, clutching Timmy's hand.

"No," Jake said firmly. "No matter what happens on a mission, you have to come back here. To the rehab center."

"But . . ."

"Look," Marco explained, "if a nurse or doctor or orderly is a Controller and notices any kids missing, they're gonna know something's up. And they'll come after you. And us."

"We'll stay," James said.

"It'll be like an undercover operation!" Collette.

Jake cleared his throat. "That's not all. Staying here might be harder than you think." He paused before going on. "We don't know how, or why, or even if it works every time. But sometimes, most times, the morphing process repairs DNA."

"What are you saying?" James demanded.

"It's possible that if some of you weren't born injured or disabled, you'll be healed," I told them. "If you are healed, would you still be willing to pretend you're disabled? At least for the duration of the war?"

James, Collette, and Kelly were silent. Their faces revealed nothing of their thoughts.

But Timmy was incapable of hiding his emotions.

"FFF . . . gnnn . . . Fff . . . gnnn . . ."

"If I can . . ." James translated.

"Do . . . gd . . . YES."

"He said 'If I can do some good, then yes.'"

Timmy rocked back and forth, confirming James's translation.

Jake turned to Collette. "What about you? Your injuries are the result of an accident. There's a good chance your body will be repaired through morphing."

Collette's hands fidgeted in her lap.

"Ummmm . . . I . . . Look. I wasn't exactly injured in a skiing accident."

Timmy shot James a look and grinned.

"I've been lying," she said.

Timmy let out a long, high note of hilarity.

Collette's face fell.

"You knew?"

"Everybody knows you've been a paraplegic since birth," James said quietly. "It's on your chart."

"Why didn't you say anything?" Collette cried.

Kelly smiled. "It's okay, Collette."

"We kind of enjoyed the tall tales," James answered. "I'm guessing we all have pretty rich fantasy lives. But yours had real style."

"Why did you lie?" I asked her.

Collete's dark eyes filled with tears.

"To ignore the reality," she said simply. "My mom died two years ago. After that, I lived with my brother and his wife. But they were transferred overseas. They're in the army. I was just supposed to be here until they got settled and sent for me. But then they wrote and said nothing was barrier free where they were stationed. It would be too hard to have me live with them. So I'm supposed to live here till they get back. It could be years."

Marco leaned over and squeezed Collette's shoulder. "It's okay," he said gently. "I've been known to stretch the truth on occasion."

"Do you still want me on the team?" she asked softly. "Even though I'm a liar?"

Jake started to answer, then looked to James.

James gave Jake a curt nod.

"Yup," Jake said.

I smiled. "Collette, you'll never have to make up stories again. The truth is going to be stranger than any fiction. Believe me."

Marco grinned. "Great. Now that we've got all that settled . . . *voilà!*" He reached into the cape and produced the pigeon.

After the show James and his friends had just witnessed, it didn't seem like much of a trick.

Especially when the pigeon pooped in Marco's hand.

# CHAPTER 17

The pigeon would give everyone an unobtrusive transit morph. Like our own seagull morphs.

Carefully we explained the acquiring trance and then how the actual morphing process would feel.

We waited for dark.

Then Jake went falcon. Marco and I went osprey.

And the new Animorphs went pigeon.

Three birds of prey perched on the roof of the rehab center and watched the wildest, wackiest, most joyful pigeon rodeo ever.

Because the minute James and the others had wings, they were — transformed.

And thought-speak? For Timmy, this was the biggest miracle.

<Rubber baby buggy bumpers. Rubber baby buggy bumpers. Rubber baby buggy bumpers,> he chanted. <This is fantastically fabulous. Fortuitously felicitous.>

Timmy laughed at his own alliterative excesses. <You want to know what hell on Earth is?> he asked.

<What?>

<Having a large vocabulary, an encyclopedic knowledge of musical theater, and a speech impediment.>

Collette landed on the tar beside me. <Flying is the coolest thing I have ever, ever done. I can't believe this is really happening!>

<You didn't mind the morphing?> I asked. <It didn't gross you out?>

<Are you kidding? After a spinal tap or two, morphing is nothing! It's, like, as easy as eating yogurt from a tube!>

<You know,> Marco noted, <if we were real birds of prey, one of us might try to eat one of you.>

Collette laughed wildly and lifted off. <You're so gross!>

<See?> Marco said. <I told you she likes me.>

<This is amazing,> Kelly cried. <It's the first time I can really breathe since I got sick.>

<Okay,> Jake called. <Time to rein it in. Re-

member, the point is not to call attention to your-selves. To act like real pigeons.>

<Everybody!> James said. <Chill.>

And they did. They listened to James without hesitation.

Then Jake formed us into a loose squadron — safe under cover of a moonless night — and we flew out to The Gardens.

<Wait till I give the signal before landing,> Jake said.

He flew a quick flyby then gave us the all-clear signal.

<Demorph,> he said to everyone. To Marco and me, he added privately, <Watch them. This is it.>

Who would be healed?

I hurried through my own demorph. Felt my human face push out through the bird's head. Beak stretch wider and wider, then simply fade into my mouth with an itchy tingle.

Osprey body wobbled as my slim bird legs stretched out to strong human legs. Center of gravity way off, I barely managed to keep my balance as the rest of my human body emerged.

Our new recruits were not so lucky.

Timmy tumbled to the grass. Lay on the ground in a sort of fetal position as the last of gray feathers retracted.

Collette supported her upper body with her arms. Stared at her legs, stretched out useless in front of her.

Kelly tried to stand, but was overtaken by a fit of coughing. Timmy reached out and gently but awkwardly pounded her back with a palsied hand.

I watched them and felt sad and sick. They were helpless out of morph, without their wheelchairs and other supports. Even more helpless than I had imagined.

Were they wondering the same thing? Regretting their decision to join us?

Nope.

Something had caught their attention.

Standing over the group now, steady and strong, was James.

He was taller than Jake. Broader-shouldered, too. He looked down at his team, and then over at Jake.

He walked in a circle, as if testing his legs. Legs that hadn't properly grown since the accident all those years before. Legs that only an hour ago had been atrophied with disuse. But that were suddenly long and muscular.

"Lucky you," Kelly whispered.

James smiled, wryly. "Yeah."

"Are you going to learn how to skateboard?" Collette.

"W . . . w . . . w . . . wiiiuuuu . . ."

"Will I stay?" James asked.

Timmy nodded, his face tense, as if he half expected James to say he wouldn't. That now he could leave the confines of the rehab center, he was going to break his promise and run for it.

James squatted so that he was face-to-face with the others.

"I'm staying. We're a team, right?" He looked up at Jake. His eyes were bright with tears. "What now?"

93

# CHAPTER 18

It was a long night.

Jake, Marco, James, and I carried Kelly, Timmy, and Collette, one by one, into the cages of some pretty cranky wild animals.

How we did it without getting hurt I'll never know. How we did it without getting caught by a guard or spotted by the Yeerks, I'll never understand. The fact that we even tried such a bold move tells you how desperate we were.

The other thing? The thing that really amazed us?

The new guys got control of the morphs almost immediately. I mean, there was no lag time at all. The animals' instincts kicked in and almost immediately, James and the others got them under control. No rampaging tempers or out-of-control panic.

I thought about that. Finally figured that James and the others had spent years — if not all of their lives — surviving by allowing mind to conquer and replace matter. Their bodies might be weak, but their wills were stronger than ours.

The new team went back to the rehab center that night. In through the windows and back under the covers before anybody knew they were missing.

We trusted them and they did us proud.

The next night, after lights-out at the rehab center, we gathered again in the private lounge. Marco's gorilla morph kept look-out while Jake explained to a new group of potential recruits — preselected by James — that the guy at the door wasn't a kid in a monkey suit but the real thing. And about the Yeerks.

On three more consecutive nights a few of us took a direct route to the rehab center to repeat the process.

Surveillance continued to reveal no Yeerk activity. As far as we could know, our plan was undiscovered.

At the end of the fifth night, Jake, Ax, and I flew back to camp where Marco, Rachel, and Tobias were waiting. Dawn was still hours away.

"That makes seventeen new recruits," Jake

said excitedly. "With the six of us, that's twenty-three Animorphs."

<In addition to the Chee and a possibly still active Yeerk resistance,> Ax added.

<And Toby's Hork-Bajir.> Tobias.

The mood was high. Not euphoric, but better than it had been in a while.

Even so, I was full of mixed emotions. Wondered if I would have the chance to know these new team members as I'd come to know — and care for — my friends. Wondered if it mattered.

Already I felt responsible for them. Like their mother. Older sister, at least.

I also wondered: *Would the Animorphs function as smoothly with twenty-three members as we had with six? With James now as a leader of the majority of members — though Jake was still in charge overall?*

*So* many questions.

Lots about the larger ramifications of what we'd done.

Yeah, sure, we'd told James and the others about the incredible dangers they faced as warriors. They'd signed on in spite of our warnings.

<When most of these new Animorphs demorph, they are physically helpless. Correct?> Ax.

"Yes," Jake answered, his voice defensive. "Except for James and two others. But at least we know they're not Controllers."

<I still must point out that does not mean they will be useful in a battle,> Ax countered. <They will have to be tested. If these new recruits have no training, no experience with the world of physical sport or combat, then they are of no use to us.>

"Look, Ax," Marco interrupted. "We've had this conversation before. This is Earth. All people are valuable in some way or another. Humans value one another. Whether they're disabled or not."

Ax blinked. <If these people are valued, then why are they kept apart? Why are they unseen? It is a disturbing inconsistency.>

Trust Ax to put his finger right on the ugly truth.

Of course, I could have pointed out that Andalite culture had its own vanities and conceits. I could have mentioned Mertil again.

But I wasn't interested in an argument. I just wanted to go to sleep and wake up to discover the whole thing had been a bad dream.

Ax nodded gravely. <Jake is the leader. He is my prince. I will trust his judgment.>

"Thanks, Ax," Jake said quietly. "That means a lot."

# CHAPTER 19

Ax handed Jake a printout. <I have located another facility.>

Marco looked at the printout over Jake's shoulder. "A school for the blind. Not far. If we go now, we could have another four or five recruits by daylight."

Jake nodded. For the first time I noticed the lines around his mouth. And that he'd lost weight.

"Let's go. The whole team this time, now that we have backup. Rachel, go eagle and carry the morphing cube. Tobias, we'll have any recruits acquire your hawk again. Unless, of course, Marco finds a seagull along the way."

Before we left Jake decided it was time to tell

Toby about our recent recruiting missions. Her reaction was hard to read.

I had a strong sense that, like me, Toby was not thrilled with our methods. But that, also like me, she'd publically endorsed and put her trust in Jake as leader. And she was nothing if not loyal.

"Be careful, Jake," she said. "I will post more guards and wait for your return."

Suddenly, a rustle of leaves.

My dad had stepped forward out of the shadows. "I couldn't sleep so I got up to get some air," he said. "And I couldn't help but overhear your conversation."

His face was gaunt and haggard in the predawn light. He seemed to have aged ten years in the last twenty-four hours.

Dad looked at me for a long time. I can't bear to describe the expression on his face.

He was looking at me like I was the enemy. Like he suddenly understood that evil existed not just in the world, not just in his own backyard, but in his very own kid. His very own flesh and blood.

"Please tell me I misunderstood," he said. "Please tell me you haven't actually convinced disabled children to participate in this nightmare."

Jake spoke. "We had no choice."

"There's always a choice," my father said angrily. "Jake, I thought you knew that. Where's the boy I used to know? The boy who was so clear on right and wrong."

I wondered the same thing.

Jake wasn't Jake anymore. His eyes were harder. Maybe his heart, too. And I didn't like the look that came over his face now.

It was the look that Rachel got when she was determined to win no matter what. It was the look Tobias got when he was closing in on a mouse.

"We'll wait for you over there," Jake told me. He didn't answer my father. He just led Toby and the others away.

Even Jake's back looked different. Straighter. More unyielding.

Jake, the Jake I knew, was going away. And I didn't know how to get him back.

Yet I still felt I had to defend him.

"Dad," I said. "I don't have time to argue ethics with you. I don't have time to convince you that sometimes you have to do something — uncomfortable — to make things right in the end. This is war. Every minute counts. We're fighting to save the human race."

"The human race?" my father repeated. "Okay, answer me this, Cassie. Is what you're doing with these disabled children humane?"

My father sounded like me.

Like the old me.

But I wasn't that naive person anymore.

I had no answer.

I turned and walked away. Started to morph osprey.

"Cassie!" he cried. "Cassie! Wait!"

But I didn't wait. I finished the morph and flew.

The others were in the trees. Rachel in bald eagle morph. Jake in peregrine falcon morph. Ax, northern harrier. Marco, an osprey like me. And Tobias a red-tailed hawk.

In the daylight, six birds of prey could never travel together. It would attract attention. But while it was still night it would be difficult to observe us. And these were our strongest and safest transit morphs.

I heard the others take wing, leave branches, and cut through the sky around me.

Our destination, the school for blind kids. Only a few miles from the rehab center.

But it seemed to me a long, long journey. Every mile dragged like ten. Every minute stretched like an hour.

My little osprey heart began to race.

What if we didn't make it back? What if the Yeerks found the camp while we were gone? What if I never had a chance to see or talk to my dad again?

Could I live with never seeing him again, re-membering the way we'd left things?

I wheeled sharply and headed back toward the camp.

Behind me, the heavy beating of falcon wings.

Jake.

<Cassie! Where are you going?>

<Back to camp,> I answered.

<What?>

<I'm going back. I can't go with you. I've got to talk to my dad.>

<You can't afford to panic. None of us can,> Jake said sternly.

<You don't understand . . .>

<Hey! You're the one who said I had to be in charge. Why are you arguing with me now?>

Birds don't cry. So I didn't. But it was only because I *couldn't.*

I was miserable.

I just wanted to protect.

Protect my parents. Protect my friends. Pro-tect the new team.

Was this how Jake felt all the time?

Probably. Yes.

How did he stand it?

No wonder he'd wanted out.

# CHAPTER 20

The school for the blind was easy to infiltrate. Fifteen-minute surveillance, during which we located the dormitory floor.

In through the ventilation system as insects, demorph in the basement, then the stairs up to the fourth floor.

Once in the hall, we paused.

"Am I the only one who's thinking it might be hard to convince kids who can't even see us?" Marco whispered.

"I thought about that," Rachel answered. "I figured Jake had a plan."

<I feel I must repeat my opinion in this matter.> Ax. <Perhaps unsighted *vecols* are not the best prospects for a new team of warriors.>

"Listen, Ax . . ."

"Shhh!" Jake said harshly.

Every eye turned to look at him. Waited for him to tell us what to do.

"Well?" Marco said. "What's the plan?"

"I'll think of something," Jake said irritably. He pushed open the door of the first room and walked in.

About twenty kids, roughly our age, were asleep in beds lined up along both sides of the wall.

Light from a street lamp glowed softly in the window, both eerie and beautiful.

"Who's there?" a voice asked softly.

At the end of the room a girl sat up in her bed. Long red hair hung over her shoulders.

Rachel tiptoed down the aisle and knelt beside the girl. "My name is Rachel," she whispered. "Uh, sorry to wake you up. But I need your help."

"What?" The girl sounded surprised but not alarmed. This was a good start.

"Don't be scared," Rachel said. "There are six of us. Me and my friends."

"What do you want?"

Jake joined Rachel by the girl's bed and began to talk softly. Ax stood guard at the door, tail blade poised. Tobias perched on a shelf by the window. Marco quietly went gorilla.

Everything seemed fine. And then, I got the

uncomfortable feeling that we were being watched.

I checked. Every kid besides the red-haired girl was asleep.

Standard-issue blue covers rose and fell with the soft breathing of the sleepers. Peaceful. Jake and Rachel were still talking to the girl. Ax, Marco, and Tobias seemed untroubled. But still . . . Maybe I was missing something.

I morphed to horned owl. Wonderful night vision.

Suddenly, every tiny detail in the room was fully visible. Gnats swarming around the dull glow of the street lamp reflected in the window.

Clouds of sparkling dust. A salamander, streaking along the baseboard. Nothing suspicious. Nobody hiding, watching.

A sharp intake of breath. Jake, morphing to tiger while the red-haired girl's hand rested on his head.

Rachel holding the girl's hand now. A dreamy look on her face.

And then it happened again. My gut screamed at me. Something was wrong. Something was very wrong.

I demorphed. Remorphed to fly.

That's when I saw it. A tiny, tiny pinpoint of infrared light. A camera was surveying the room!

<The room is being watched!> I shouted.

105

Too late!

The door flew open. Ten Blue Band Hork-Bajir-Controllers stormed in. Overwhelmed Ax before he could react. Aimed Dracon beams at Tobias and Marco.

Chaos!

Kids sat up in bed. Some screamed. Some shouted questions. "What's happening? Who's there? What's going on?"

"Nothing to worry about." A human voice. "Just some pranksters."

The Hork-Bajir stood aside. And in walked Tom.

Tom. Jake's brother. A human-Controller.

Tom walked up the aisle. Toward Jake, fully human again.

"Some mean kids have broken in to play a practical joke," Tom said, grinning. "But it's not funny and we're going to throw them out right now."

Tom grabbed Jake's arm.

Jake hissed a command to Rachel. She stepped back, her face a mask of fury.

Jake didn't resist.

Neither did Marco. Tobias. Ax. They couldn't. Not with all those innocent kids in the room.

Tom opened his other hand, palm out. "Give it to me."

Jake didn't move.

Tom wrenched Jake's arm. Yanked him closer. "Give it to me. Now."

Slowly, without taking his eyes off Tom, Jake reached into his pocket. Pulled out the blue morphing cube. Placed it in Tom's hand.

Tom closed his fingers around the cube. Grinned.

"Okay," he said. "Let's all leave quietly."

Two Hork-Bajir-Controllers stood like sentries. The other eight marched Jake and the others into the hall.

<I'm following, Jake,> I said. Knowing he could hear but not answer me.

<Cassie?> Marco. <If it comes to it, get James.>

When we were in the hallway, Tom closed the door behind us. Then he turned and struck Jake savagely across the face. "My host's own brother!"

Jake reeled and a Hork-Bajir caught him. Propped him up.

Tom struck him again. "Do you have any idea what you've done to me? All that time we were searching for *you*. Looking for Andalites. And it was you! Right there in my own house. Right down the hall. I could have killed you a million times! Visser One almost starved me to death for my stupidity."

Rachel's face was red with fury. Frustration.

Ax's stalk eyes were blank. His tail held by a smirking Hork-Bajir.

Marco was still, a Dracon beam pointed at his skull. Tobias was gripped under a Hork-Bajir arm.

This was worse than it had ever been.

Still Jake said nothing. His face was unreadable.

"Take them down to the garage off the loading dock," Tom ordered the Hork-Bajir Controllers. "If the girl tries to morph or escape, kill her. Make the gorilla and the bird demorph. Keep the Andalite under extra guard. He'll make a special host body. And inform Visser One that we have the rebels. And the cube."

Tom turned back to Jake. "My host's parents," he said coldly, "were given as hosts to relatively low-ranking Controllers. This is so we can kill them without regret if we have to. So if any of you even thinks about making trouble . . ."

# CHAPTER 21

When they'd gone I moved from my still place above the door. I had to get to a window, get out, demorph! With the crazy, zigzagging, up-and-down antics of the fly I made it to a hall window. Zipped through a narrow opening, down to the ground.

Demorphed and remorphed to owl under cover of a low-hanging tree and in record time.

Up up up! I flew to the rehab center. Tried desperately not to think about what might be happening to Jake. Knew that if we didn't stop Tom before he left the school we'd have to infiltrate the Yeerk pool. Me, James, and the new teams.

And that was something I was seriously hoping to avoid.

No time to worry about being subtle. In through James's open window. Heavy landing on the foot of his bed.

<James. We need you. Now!>

James threw back the covers and jumped out of bed.

The owl's keen eyes saw Pedro's flickering with wonder. James leaned over his friend. "I'll explain later," he whispered. "I promise I'll be back."

Then he threw himself into his wheelchair. I hopped onto his lap and he tossed a blanket over me. We wheeled into the hallway. Nipped into one room, and then another.

Moments later, the new Animorphs were assembled in Timmy's room.

All seventeen of them.

I hopped off James's lap and demorphed.

Timmy pulled himself up to a sitting position. "Sss . . . s . . ."

"Yes," James agreed with a smile. He surveyed the group of kids he'd chosen to join the fight. "It is soon. But we knew things were really serious."

James motioned to a boy named Craig. A girl named Erica. Like James, they'd been healed by the morphing process. Like James, they were pretending to still need care. How they managed it, I don't know.

Craig and Erica were, in effect, James's lieutenants.

"Get everyone in transit morphs," James instructed. "We'll follow Cassie to the school."

Briefly I gave directions. Instructed everyone to gather in the wooded area at the rear of the building. Just outside the large metal door to the loading dock and garage.

For a moment, the new Animorphs froze. Every one of them. Then, with the encouragement of James, Craig, and Erica, they burst into excited motion.

And I found myself in a room with a variety of animals. Not all of them birds.

There was a baboon, a walrus, and a hedgehog.

<NO!> James yelled.

<I couldn't help it,> Kelly wailed. <The minute I thought about a walrus, I was one.>

"You've got to focus," I said. "Remember what you're trying to do. Keep your mind on your morph."

<Okay! Let's all try again,> James urged. <Pigeons. Okay? Think feathers.>

This time, they got it. Within minutes I was a girl among a strange flock of pigeons and red-tailed hawks.

I couldn't help it. I felt so proud.

I morphed back to owl. Led the way to the

school for the blind. Reminding everyone to keep watch, act like the bird.

About a half mile from our destination, I spotted a long black limo speeding along with a police escort.

<James, that's probably Visser One. Hurry!> Eighteen Animorphs landed in the wooded area behind the loading dock. Visser One was only minutes away.

<Now what?> James.

<Now comes the hard part.> How could I lie? How could I say everything was going to be all right — when it wasn't?

<Listen everyone!> I shouted. <Behind that door are Hork-Bajir-Controllers. They're going to scare you to death. They're going to have weapons, too. But you have to fight them. You have to fight them and you have to win.>

<But we don't know how to fight!> One of Erica's team. A girl named Jessie.

<Are we supposed to use, like, weapons?> A boy named Liam. One of Craig's team. <I'm pretty opposed to guns.>

Then Timmy spoke. <James, I've never had a fight in my life. Who's going to throw down with a kid in a wheelchair?>

<He's got a point. They all do,> Erica said. <We don't know anything about tactics. We're

not used to thinking about winning over other people. About strategizing.>

My heart began to sink. This was not going to work! And Jake was waiting for us, for me.

"Everyone, just listen!" James had demorphed. It was a good move on his part. His healthy body radiated confidence and strength. "Yes, you do know how to fight," he said furiously. "You do know how to win. People like us fight and win every minute of every day."

<That's different!> Kelly argued. <It's what we do to survive. You know it is.>

"Okay!" James admitted. "But even if our daily lives aren't about knocking out the bad guys, our Animorphs lives are. Look, we made a promise. The place is here and the time is now. Ready or not, we're doing this. Everybody, demorph!"

A small miracle. The new Animorphs overcame their reluctance, their fear. And began to demorph.

Kelly's tiny bird skull expanded. Tiny black bird eyes sunk into now-human eye sockets.

And as soon as her human chest emerged, she began to cough.

Timmy's human legs shot out from his torso, rocketing him off the ground. But they were far too weak to support his now completely human body. With a cry of alarm he tumbled to the ground. I heard his head make contact with a rock.

Collette had demorphed with relatively little difficulty. Now she dragged herself across the ground toward Timmy. His forehead was bleeding.

My own demorph had been unproblematic. But looking at these new recruits, my fingertips went numb. These physically disabled, incredibly brave kids were about to wade into battle.

They wouldn't make it.

James strode over to Timmy, examined his forehead. "You'll be okay," he said.

Timmy nodded. He lifted his jerking hand to feel the wound himself.

The gesture went straight to my heart. I didn't want these kids to get hurt.

Why hadn't I listened to my dad? How could we have done something so irresponsible? So stupid! So cruel. We — the Animorphs — were as bad as the Yeerks.

We were worse than the Yeerks!

I grasped James's arm. "It's okay. We can handle it without you. Morph to bird and get everyone out of here. Fly away as fast as you can!"

"No, Cassie." James looked down at me. Gently squeezed the hand that held his arm.

"They won't make it, James. They can't."

James smiled and stepped away. "Watch us." To the others: "Battle morphs. Now."

Kelly. Streaks of dark black puddled around her face. Her nose flattened, turned large and pink. Two horns sprouted from her head.

Within seconds she was a charging, snorting bull.

Collette. Her arms shortened. Legs retracted and bent. Snout stretched. Black-green skin appeared along the bridge of her nose, coursed down the length of her body. She was a crocodile.

Timmy's shoulders hunched, rounded out. His forehead shrank, chin retracted. Body turned sleek and muscled. Short tan fur sprouted from nose to tail. Sharp teeth erupted from the bottom and top gums. He was a bobcat.

All around me, warriors. A gorilla, after Marco's favorite morph. Another elephant. In spite of Rachel's jealousy, a grizzly, chosen by a boy named Julio. Rattlesnake, rhino, wolf, panther, golden eagle.

James's choice of battle morph was an ironic one. Though when he'd chosen a male lion, he had no idea David, the ill-fated Animorph, had chosen the same.

Jake is not superstitious. Ignoring our meaningful looks, he'd said nothing. Except, "Good choice, James."

Now, watching the lion's wild golden mane emerge from James's own thick golden hair, the morph seemed somehow appropriate.

<We're going in, Cassie,> he said. <With or without you. Are you going to help us?>

I nodded, closed my eyes, and went wolf.

# CHAPTER 22

A concrete ramp led toward the loading dock and the wide metal garage door.

We gathered at the bottom of the ramp.

James, in lion morph, addressed the entire team.

<Okay. We're going to do this. And we're not disabled anymore. We don't need to wait for people to open doors. Kelly, knock it down and let's rock and roll.>

Kelly backed up, snorted, and pawed the ground.

And then she charged up the ramp, hooves thundering. When her massive skull met the metal door, it crumpled.

WHAM!

She backed away. Let Judy, in elephant morph, ram the door again. This time, it gave way.

And there they were.

Tom, his battalion of Hork-Bajir, and the Animorphs.

Jake was alive. Blood trickled from his forehead, but he was alive.

<Go go go!> James yelled.

Kelly charged three Hork-Bajir standing side by side.

BLAM!

Knocked them down like bowling pins.

Tseeeew! Tseeeew!

Three other Hork-Bajir fanned out, Dracon beams firing.

Collette shot forward with the crocodile's unexpected speed. Her thick muscular tail thrashed Hork-Bajir ankles. One fell hard on his rump. Another growled and slashed, leaving a long gash along the crocodile's back. Not deep enough to do any serious damage. But Collette was our first casualty.

<Don't worry, Collette!> I shouted. <It'll heal when you demorph!>

Collette snapped her jaws and shot back into the fray.

<Who wants to wrestle this big green baby!> she cried.

Maybe extreme sports really were her thing.

Tom lifted his arm. Pointed a gun straight at Timmy.

<Look out!> James commanded.

<I've got him!>

And with incredible grace, Timmy gathered the bobcat's muscular legs beneath him and leaped.

"Ooof!"

Tom was knocked to the ground. The bobcat bounded off his chest. Clamped down on Tom's wrist until he released the gun. Batted it into the shadows with his paw.

And then the morphing cube rolled from Tom's shirt pocket.

James darted forward and grabbed the morphing cube in his teeth.

"Stop him!" Tom shrieked.

He struggled to sit up but Timmy bounded back onto his chest.

Jake and the others had ducked behind a wall of boxes and morphed. Ax had broken free of his captor, who now had one less arm. Tobias morphed then went back to red-tailed hawk.

Just in time, too.

I spun around. Through the hole left by the destroyed door I saw a long black limo hurtle to a stop.

The doors opened.

Visser One emerged in his human form. And immediately demorphed to Andalite.

A moving truck pulled up behind the limo.

Then another.

The doors to the first moving truck opened and another battalion of Hork-Bajir clambered out.

The doors of the second moving truck opened and out poured a mob of Taxxons. No doubt eager for fresh kill.

Visser One clumped up the ramp. Timmy slunk into the shadows, leaving Tom still sprawled on the floor.

<Where is the morphing cube?> Visser One demanded.

No greetings. No formalities or preliminaries. Tom's mouth quivered nervously. Slowly he got to his feet; his eyes remained on the visser. "It's here. Somewhere. The lion got it and . . ."

<So!> the visser roared. <You have failed again. This is the last time. If the bandits do not kill you, I will kill you myself.>

"I had it! I had the morphing cube," Tom cried. "It was in my hand!"

<Then your failure is even less forgivable!> Visser One spat.

<James!>

He'd rejoined us.

<The cube is okay,> he said.

<Someone needs to get it,> Jake snapped. <It shouldn't be out of our sight. Let's move out.>

Slowly our team formed a line. Grizzly. Gorilla. Tiger. Andalite. Hawk. Wolf.

Then James's team. Lion. Crocodile. Bobcat. Bull.

Then Craig's team. And Erica's.

Slowly the visser's attention was caught. Maybe I imagined the look of fear that flitted across his enigmatic Andalite face as he surveyed our forces.

Maybe not.

But for the first time since this war had begun, it looked like a fair fight.

# CHAPTER 23

Teamwork seemed to come easily to the new Animorphs.

This was a good thing.

"Rrrrooooooow!"

Timmy leaped at a Hork-Bajir's head. Collette chomped on the Hork-Bajir's leg.

"Gaaallaaafff!"

The Hork-Bajir toppled over backward, blades whisking the air. Timmy and Collette hurried on to their next target. Leaving the fallen, bloody Hork-Bajir to defend himself against a voracious Taxxon.

"Hhhhrrrooowwwrrr!"

James! The mind-boggling roar of the lion filled the garage, threatening to burst the walls.

James batted a Taxxon with his massive paw. Guts spilled from the long wounds his claws had torn. Then he turned, leaped on a Hork-Bajir, sunk his teeth into the leathery neck until the Hork-Bajir lay still. Suffocated. Its throat bit out.

Kelly helped Marco clear a path through looming Taxxons. Horns punctured their baglike bodies, sending the foul contents spilling to the ground. Bulk and muscle shoved the remains out of our path.

<Yes!> Rachel. <Kick butt, folks. This is your chance!>

Slowly but surely James led his team further into the garage. Followed closely by Craig's and Erica's teams. Slashing, snapping, biting. Plowing through Taxxons, ducking Hork-Bajir blades, skidding on pooling blood.

<Andalite scum!> Visser One twitched his tail blade over his head, taunting Ax. <You will make a lovely host for some worthy Yeerk. That is, if you survive the next few minutes.>

Fwap!

Ax easily evaded the intended blow.

<You are losing your touch, Visser,> Ax sneered.

Jake turned and joined Ax.

<So! It takes two rebel scum to fight me!>

<Your boasting is foolish,> Ax retorted. <You

have brought truckloads of troops to fight only a few of us.>

Again, Visser One swung his blade at Ax's throat. It missed by inches.

Jake gathered his legs beneath him and leaped. Landed briefly on Visser One's back. Dug in his claws, then launched off.

Visser One cursed and whirled. Stumbled and recovered.

<Is it my imagination,> he said, trying to sound unconcerned, <or are there more of you rebels this time?>

<There are many of us,> Jake lied. <There always have been.>

<Tell me how many and I will let you live,> Visser One coaxed. All four eyes alert.

<Release Tom's host's parents and I will let *you* live,> Jake countered.

<Your arrogance is entertaining. Of course I know the tiger is Tom's brother. Let me tell you, human, you will regret your arrogance. You will regret it all.>

And then Visser One began to morph. I had to warn the others. This fight was about to turn even uglier.

I backed away.

Tseeeeew! Tseeeeew!

Dracon fire from all directions.

Screams, cries, moans.

Blood spraying . . .

<Everyone! Remember to get away and de-morph if you're hurt!> I shouted.

Tseeeeew! Tseeeeew!

I had to find James. Stood on the wolf's back paws.

That's when I saw Tom. Up on a pile of wood planks stacked against the wall. Pointing a Dracon beam!

Tseeeew!

A beam struck Kelly in the shoulder. She let out a roar of rage and and turned the massive bull's head to see who had fired on her.

<Kelly, no!>

Too late!

A Taxxon butted her from the side! Her legs buckled beneath her and she went down. The Taxxon sunk the needlelike teeth of its red maw into the bull's flesh.

<I'm coming, Kelly!> I cried.

A Hork-Bajir extended an arm blade, attempting to slice me across the chest. To stop me. I jumped over the blade as if it were a bar.

The Taxxon was still bent over Kelly, foul saliva trickling onto her flesh. Sucking up the bull's dark blood.

Marco! Slamming his gorilla body into the

Taxxon! Sending it sprawling into the Hork-Bajir who had tried to stop me. The Taxxon impaled itself on the Hork-Bajir's blades.

<Hang in, Kelly,> Marco cried.

<I'm . . . I'm bleeding,> she whispered.

Understatement. The wound caused by the Dracon beam was worse than I'd thought. And the Taxxon had opened a massive area of flesh. Kelly was losing blood and strength rapidly.

<Can you stand?> I asked.

"Grraaaath!" A Hork-Bajir, lumbering at us, blades up.

<I got this one.>

Marco roared. The Hork-Bajir skidded to a stop, confused.

<Get up, Kelly!>

With a groan of effort, Kelly climbed to her feet.

<I can't . . .>

And fell heavily.

She was hurt. She needed to demorph.

Or she would die.

# CHAPTER 24

Visser One was now a giant squidlike creature. A fat body covered with gleaming black scales. Raw red eyes bulged from dark flesh. Twenty massive, spike-covered tentacles whirled and cracked in the air like bullwhips.

I nudged Kelly's prone body. She was alive, but barely. And the only thing keeping the Taxxons at bay was Marco.

WHAP!

A tree-trunklike tentacle swept a path through the battle.

Rachel stepped into the clearing. Charged!

Jake joined her.

"Tsseeeer!"

127

From another direction . . .

Tobias!

"Aaaaah!"

Tom clutched his face. Blood gushed through his fingers. He dropped to his knees.

Swaaaap!

The visser!

A spiky tentacle snapped against Rachel's shoulder. With a roar of rage she stumbled to her knees.

Swaaaap!

Another tentacle, wrapped around Jake's neck like a lasso! Like a rope of thorns.

<James!> I cried. <The visser's got Jake!>

Jake planted his paws wide. Jerked his head right then left. Madly trying to loosen the visser's grip.

Slowly, inevitably, he was dragged closer to the visser.

Slowly, inevitably, the entire battle moved inward, toward Visser One and his captive. Taxxons and Hork-Bajir surged forward. Some continued to fight the Animorphs. Others formed a ring of spectators, eager to see the leader of the bandits defeated at last.

No one paid any attention to us. Now was the time to get Kelly out.

<Kelly! Can you hear me?>

<I'm sorry,> she gasped.

<For what?> I said. <But you've got to de-morph.>

<No! I'll die. They'll kill me.>

<You're dying now,> I said. <Demorph then remorph.>

<I can't! If they see me . . . they'll know who I am. They'll figure everything out. And then everyone will be in danger.>

<Don't think about that,> I cried. <While their backs are turned. Marco can carry you out.>

Her eyes closed. She didn't answer.

<Kelly! Can you hear me?>

Still no answer.

The wolf yearned to lift its head and let out a long, heartbroken howl of anguish.

Then: <Cassie!> Marco whispered. <She's doing it. She's demorphing.>

It was true.

The bull began to shrivel. As if it were a paper-and-cardboard bull that had been left in the rain. The muscle and hide crumpled. Collapsed until it appeared to be a wet blanket of smudged newspaper, covering a small, frail body.

Moments later, Kelly lay on the ground completely demorphed, gasping for air.

<Good work!> Marco said, easily lifting her in his arms.

He ran with Kelly, away from the garage. Out into the safety of the dark and shadows.

<I'll be back,> he cried.

The rest of us might not make it out. If we didn't, and the Yeerks won the planet, someone somewhere needed to know the truth. That some ordinary and some very extraordinary kids had tried to stop the madness.

Screams and guttural cheers.

I turned.

Visser One was taunting Jake. Curling the tentacle to pull him closer. Whipping him through the air. Smacking him on the floor.

The tiger's head and neck were a bloody mess. Jake wouldn't survive this torture much longer.

One by one, the Animorphs snuck in close. Rushed the big black body. Sliced or bit. But each time they were knocked back by a wild tentacle.

James. Rachel. Timmy. Ax.

"Tsseeer!"

Tobias! Streaking past Visser One's distorted face. Talons poised to gouge the oozing red eyes.

<No!>

The monster's huge spiny tongue darted out like yet another bullwhip. Smacked Tobias dead on. Sent him flying across the room.

Tobias hit a metal wall! Fell to the ground in a crumpled pile of feathers.

<Tobias!> I ran to his inert body. Awkwardly picked him up with my mouth.

He was alive. I could feel his heartbeat against my teeth and lips. Once we were out of sight, he could demorph and remorph and he'd be fine.

I would go back in. I would fight to the finish. No matter what, I'd fight with Jake.

I dropped Tobias on the ground as soon as we were out of sight. He was already demorphing.

<Go back to camp,> I told him, voice breaking. <Tell them to be ready to evacuate.>

# CHAPTER 25

Jake was down, on his back, the visser's tentacle wrapped firmly around his throat.

<Where is the morphing cube?> the visser roared.

No response.

Visser One tightened his grip. A small, pitiful sound erupted from Jake's throat. The tiger's windpipe was being crushed.

Rachel lunged. James roared.

Visser One's punishing tentacles sent each one sprawling.

<*Where* is the morphing cube?> Visser One demanded.

Jake was dying in front of my eyes.

And at that moment . . .

"ARGHHGHGHGH!" Visser One let out an enraged howl of pain.

The tentacle that held Jake prisoner had been neatly severed.

Jake leaped to his feet. Slowly shook off the dead piece of flesh around his neck.

Visser One waved a bleeding stump in the air.

The crowd of Hork-Bajir shifted nervously, eyeing one another. Which one had done it?

It could mean only one thing. The Yeerk resistance was not dead! Somewhere, in the ranks of the assembled Hork-Bajir-Controllers, was a fellow freedom fighter.

And he had saved Jake.

Before the Hork-Bajir could attempt to ferret out the traitor among them, mayhem erupted.

Taxxons, unable to restrain their appetites, converged on Visser One and his hemorrhaging stump.

The loyal Hork-Bajir-Controllers tried to beat them back. Protect Visser One so that he could demorph safely.

And while the Taxxons, Hork-Bajir, and Visser One were engaged, Jake gave the order to bail.

<Everyone! Get out!>

James repeated the order. And the Animorphs began to stream into the night.

We would live. But . . .

The morphing cube!

<Jake!> I cried privately. <The morphing cube! I'll . . .>

I stopped in my tracks.

Because there stood Tom, unsteady, blood dried and streaked on his face. Clutching the blue box. And a Dracon beam.

His eyes were wild. They darted toward Visser One. I imagined what Tom was thinking. Whoever had the morphing cube held the future of the planet in his hands.

Why should he hand that over to Visser One?

Tom ran.

I followed him to the edge of the ramp. Saw a pair of eyes gleaming in the dark below me. A crouched body, black and orange.

Jake!

He watched as Tom staggered past. Then padded after him. His paws nearly silent.

Again, I followed. Into the surrounding woods. Beyond sight of the school. Barely keeping Jake, the silent, bloody beast, in sight.

Still, Tom must have sensed something. Because suddenly he looked over his shoulder. Turned.

And fired.

The Dracon beam singed Jake's shoulder! But he kept moving forward. Toward Tom.

"Back off!" Tom screamed. "I mean it, I'll kill you!"

Jake took another step forward.

Tsseeeew!

Tom fired again. The shot hit Jake in the back leg. He fell heavily.

Tom took off running. Sure that Jake would not, could not, follow.

But Jake lifted the tiger's seven-hundred-pound body on three legs and started after his brother.

Into the shadows. Into the darkest place Jake had ever been. The place where he would have to kill his brother. Or be killed by him.

Suddenly, I remembered my father's face. His voice. "Is what you're doing humane?"

No matter which way it went between Jake and Tom, I would lose Jake.

Because if Jake had to kill Tom, he'd never be the same. He would cross whatever line it was that separated us from them.

And I was pretty sure there was no crossing back.

I ran ahead into the dark. Followed the trail of Jake's blood.

Tom crashing through the woods ahead of me.

Soft, irregular thudding. Jake.

Stalking his brother. Prepared to kill him. For what?

For a morphing cube. For . . .

It wasn't worth it.

Suddenly, I knew the truth.

I reached the clearing where they both stood.

Tom was out of breath. Staggering.

Jake was only a yard or two behind him.

Tom turned. Lifted his arm. Aimed his weapon.

"I'll kill you, Jake," he said, voice ragged. "I will."

Jake snarled. Crouched. Prepared to spring.

That's when I shot forward and closed my jaws over Jake's uninjured back leg. Clamped down.

Jake roared. Turned on me. Smacked at my head with his paw. The blow sent me sprawling. Claws raked deep gashes in my side.

But it was worth it. The pain, everything.

I'd done what I had to do.

I'd made the sacrifice.

Tom disappeared into the night.

Jake and I lay there, panting with pain and fatigue.

We had nothing to show for this fight. Except that we were alive to fight another day.

And tomorrow, Jake could face himself in the mirror.

# CHAPTER 26

The new team made it safely back to the re-hab center and into bed without being missed.

Everyone, including Kelly.

James reported that all was well. No one wanted out. No one was threatening to talk.

If Jake thought he was losing his nose for leadership, he was wrong. James was a good pick. If we went down, there was still a home team for the human race.

The blind red-haired girl who had been observed on infrared camera talking to Jake and Rachel had escaped. Before the Yeerks could come back for her, she'd simply walked out of the facility in Rachel morph.

And the original six of us?

Were we still a team?

I didn't know. We'd been back twelve hours and Jake still hadn't spoken to me. Hadn't even looked at me.

Nobody but the two of us knew what had happened. They knew only that Tom had gotten away with the morphing cube. That Jake was devastated.

And they knew something was very wrong between me and Jake. But they didn't know why.

Finally, I decided to force the issue with Jake.

Jake stared at me, his eyes cold and hard. "Well?"

"Stop treating me like I'm the enemy," I said.

Jake turned and began to stalk away. I trotted alongside him and grabbed his sleeve.

He yanked it out of my grasp and faced me. His face was white with anger. His lips were shaking. "How could you do it?" he cried, his voice breaking. "Why?"

I choked. "I was trying to protect you!"

"Protect *me*?" His brows lifted in amazement. "How?"

"You were wounded. He might have killed you."

"Then why didn't you go after him?" Jake demanded. "You weren't hurt. With the trees for cover and the wolf's speed, you could have taken him down!"

I couldn't explain. Because I didn't under-stand it myself. All I knew was that letting Tom take the morphing cube had seemed absolutely the right thing to do.

And something still told me I was right.

## Don't miss

# #51 The Absolute

<Okay. Good.> I squinted in the semidarkness. The train had stopped. <We're safe.>

<Uh-huh.> Tobias flapped up onto a metal box. <Sealed inside a tin can, with Yeerk-infested birds nesting on top, waiting for reinforcements who will peel the lid off and kill us. We're not safe, Marco. We're dead.>

<Dead? I think not. You underestimate the power of this particular tin can.> I patted the mesh wall behind me.

The inside of the turret was a round metal basket. Everything in it — walls, floor, storage bins, equipment — had been painted white. Seats and storage bins filled the front and middle. My knees banged against a big metal box. An ammo rack jabbed my shoulder.

The tank just wasn't built for a gorilla.

I demorphed and climbed into one of the

seats. I peered through the vision block mounted above me. It was the gunner's site. Computerized. Equipped with night vision and infrared sensors. Just like the video game.

I could see the eagles and falcons. They were perched on the hull of the tank, waiting. The railroad guys were hiking along the tracks, searching the cars, searching under the cars, searching the trees. One of them was carrying the sledgehammer. Both of them looked really confused and a little ticked off.

I climbed from my seat. Stood in the center of the basket and tried to figure out what to do first.

"I assume we'll be taking this buggy for a joyride." Tobias had morphed into his human self. "If we can figure out how to start it."

"What do you mean, *if* we can figure out how to start it? You happen to be sitting next to the Tank Commando master of the Hork-Bajir valley."

"Right. Video-game expertise." He glanced around at the switches and levers. "So, what, we just rev it up and barrel off the side of the train?"

"Yeah. The train's stopped. The ground's almost level with the flatcar. Should be easy. I saw a tank crew do it on the History Channel."

"Ah. Video games and cable. How reassuring." He pulled a helmet from a hook on the side of the turret. "I should probably wear this."

"Probably. That piece in front is a microphone," I said. "And the ear thingies are speakers."

The mike was attached to a thick wire that curved down from the side of the helmet, like a telephone headset. Tobias adjusted it in front of his mouth.

"I feel like Britney Spears," he said.

"Unfortunately for me, you don't look like her. Sit here. Plug the cord in and push that little switch forward so you can talk to me."

I climbed through the crawl space between the turret and the driver's area. Everything down there was painted white, too. I slid into the seat. It tipped back so far I was almost lying down. I slipped my helmet on. Plugged it in.

And took a deep breath.

I'll let you in on a little secret. Gunning down enemy troops in a video game does not actually prepare you to operate a real-life, sixty-ton tank. I mean, yeah, the controls looked familiar. I gripped the handlebar in front of me. And the equipment was all in basically the same spots as it was on my PlayStation screen.

But this was the real deal. If I flipped the tank over, I couldn't hit ESCAPE and start again.

"How's it going down there?" Tobias's voice crackled into my helmet.

"Cool." I studied the instrument panel. "Everything's cool. Got it all figured out."

Which, I realized, was almost true. Because here's another little secret: Tank controls are amazingly well-marked. FUEL. START. MASTER SWITCH. It didn't take a genius to figure out how to get it rolling.

Was the army aware of this? Did they realize that, with a little trial and error, a third grader with a limited vocabulary could probably steal an entire tank?

I settled back into my seat. Pushed MASTER SWITCH. Heard a little hum as the instrument panel lit up.

I peered through my vision block. It wasn't a whiz-bang computerized periscope like the gunner's sight. It was more like a window. A slit of a window fitted with thick, bulletproof glass. The eagles and falcons were still perched on the tank. And they obviously knew something was up. They fluttered their feathers and stared at each other.

I pushed START.

RrrrrRRRRRRrrrrrrmmmmmm.

The engine spun up and fired. Out on the hull, our friends the birds screeched and flapped their wings.

Okay. I could do this. I gripped the handlebar thing. Right grip, throttle. Left grip, transmission. Gear switch under my left thumb.

I took a breath. In about a minute we'd either

be off the flatcar, ripping over the hills, or we'd be flipped over on the rail bed, like a big old metal bug on its back.

I kept the transmission in neutral and turned the handlebar a sharp left, it was sort of like riding my bike. Sort of. Revved the throttle. The tank rotated sideways on the bed of the flatcar. Its treads hung out over the edge, facing the cutout section of hill.

I straightened the handlebar. Shifted to drive. Pulled back on the throttle.

And we lunged forward into empty space.

The front of the treads rolled over the edge of the flatcar, supported by nothing. I could see level ground ahead. I held the throttle steady.

The tank tipped, nose down. The falcons and eagles bailed. They obviously had no confidence in my tank-driving abilities.

"Uh, Marco?" Neither, apparently, did Tobias.

WHOOOOOOMPH!

The tracks hit solid ground.

The tank hung halfway on the flatcar, half on the cutout part of the hill.

Then the treads grabbed onto the dirt and pulled us from the flatcar. We crawled across the cleared area next to the tracks. I found an opening in the line of trees, and we rattled off through the woods.

"Cake," I said.

I was very impressed with the tank. And, of course, myself. The M-1 clipped right along. It was a tank, but it could move. Anywhere. Up hills, over boulders, across ditches.

I bounced along in the driver's seat. Bushes crumbled and disappeared under my treads. Okay, and a couple of trees, too. And the corner of a railroad storage shed. It took me a while to get used to the steering.

The bird-Controllers had settled back onto the tank, their talons locked around hinges and handles, their wings bowed down against the hull.

My helmet crackled. "Call me crazy," said Tobias, "but when we abort a mission, I don't think we should bring the Yeerks home with us."

I heard a rattle above and behind me. The tank's big gun whipped to the front of the tank. Knocked a golden eagle out cold. He fell from the tank. The gun swung to the rear and then around to the front again. The other birds took to the skies.

"Tobias? That was you, wasn't it?"

"Yeah. I found an operating manual back here. Pretty dry reading, but there's some stuff in it we can definitely use."

We thundered across a clearing. Slogged through a stream. Climbed the steep bank on the other side like it was downhill. Rattled through the underbrush and back into the trees. The bird-Controllers swooped overhead.

Tobias spun the gun again. The eagles and falcons screeched and flapped toward the sky.

I thundered along, the turret basket whirling inches behind my head, trying not to get the gun tube stuck in the side of a hill or caught in a tree.

Trying to keep my eyes focused through the vision block. The woods flashed by in a blur.

THUNNNNNG.

The tank tipped sideways. Kept rolling. Thumped back to level ground.

"This is way cooler than a tank sim," said Tobias. "Think Jake'd let us keep an M-1 up in the . . . Marco! Watch out!!"

"Watch what? I can't see very well."

"I know. But I can. Stop. Stop!"

I pushed down on the brake. The tank jerked to a stop. I bounced forward, then back. I peered through my vision block.

And all I saw was sky. Acres and acres of empty air. We'd left the woods and were perched on the edge of a cliff overlooking the Interstate.

The falcons and eagles had disappeared. Smart birds.

My helmet sputtered. "Uh, Marco? Does this thing have reverse?"

I glanced at the gear switch. "Yeah."

I pressed the switch with my thumb. Gave it gas. The tank started to roll. Forward.

"AAAAAAAAAAHHHHHH!" Tobias screamed in my ear.

I slammed on the brake. The tank stopped. Chunks of earth crumbled beneath the treads and plummeted from the cliff.

"Not reverse," I said.

"No kidding."

I pressed the gear switch again. Twisted the throttle toward me a fraction of a centimeter.

The tank inched backward.

I cranked the throttle. Backed to the edge of the woods. Sat in the shadow of the trees and let the tank idle.

The "cliff" was a hill the highway department had blasted through when they built the Interstate. It sloped down on either side till it was level with the road.

I cranked the handlebar. Turned the tank. We thundered down the hill. I turned again. Plowed through the ditch and up onto the highway.

"Uh, Marco? You sure you know what you're doing?" Tobias said.

"Sure. This puppy can do sixty-five, no sweat."

"Yeah, sixty-five in the wrong direction!"

I stared out at the highway. It was divided,

with a concrete barrier between the two sides. And our side was going the wrong way.

Not much I could do about that but keep going. And hope the other vehicles were smart enough to get out of the way.

They were.

A brand-new Lexus shrieked off to the side of the road. A rusty old pickup filled with wood planks followed it.

A minivan driven by a soccer-mom skidded after them. An SUV driven by a guy in a suit swerved right behind.

So far, everyone was working with us.

Except for the eighteen-wheeler.

It kept on barreling toward us. I slowed down. Veered toward the shoulder. Plowed over a bank of road signs. Veered back onto the highway to avoid a stalled-out jeep.

Still the truck bore down on us. We were close enough now so I could see the driver's face. He was smiling. No, he was laughing.

"Is the guy a total idiot?" Tobias cried. "He's playing chicken with a tank. A tank!"

"He is bigger."

"Yeah? Well, we're better equipped."

The big gun rattled. Swung to the right.

"You can't shoot him, Tobias!"

"He doesn't know that."

The cannon rattled again. Up, this time. Straight at the truck's window.

The trucker's smile froze. He cranked his steering wheel and swerved into the next lane.

"That'll learn him," I muttered.

# Caught Off Guard!

# ANIMORPHS

## K. A. Applegate

The Yeerks have taken over units of the National Guard in preparation for an all-out war on Earth. The Animorphs couldn't be less prepared. They're living with the free Hork-Bajir colony, Jake is depressed, and worst of all, the morphing cube is in the hands of the enemy.

Marco and the others decide to approach the governor—but they don't know if she's a Controller or not. If she is, they're walking right into the enemy's hands. If she's not, the Animorphs may have to go public with their secret. And no one knows which situation would be worse.

# ANIMORPHS #51:
# THE ABSOLUTE

Coming to Bookstores this March

Watch ANIMORPHS on NICKELODEON TV